She felt his fingertips brush the nape of her neck

Linzi's breathing seemed to stop. She began to shake. It was all over in a flash; he removed her jacket in one deft movement and hung it neatly over the back of her chair, then he went back to his own chair and sat down again. Their eyes met across the table. Ritchie was as flushed as she was and his eyes looked dark, smouldering like coals.

Had he noticed what had just happened to her? She didn't even like him! He disturbed her, made her jumpy.

He had felt something, too—she was sure of that. She had known when she looked into those darkened eyes of his. He had felt something....

CHARLOTTE LAMB is one of Harlequin's best-loved and bestselling authors. Her extraordinary career has helped shape the face of romance fiction around the world.

Born in the East End of London, Charlotte spent her early childhood moving from relative to relative to escape the bombings of World War II. After working as a secretary in the BBC's European department, she married a political reporter who wrote for the *Times*. Charlotte recalls that it was at his suggestion that she began to write, "because it was one job I could do without having to leave our children." Charlotte and her family now live on the Isle of Man.

Books by Charlotte Lamb

HARLEQUIN PRESENTS PLUS

1560—SLEEPING PARTNERS
1584—FORBIDDEN FRUIT
1672—FALLING IN LOVE
1687—WOUNDS OF PASSION

HARLEQUIN PRESENTS

1480—SHOTGUN WEDDING
1618—DREAMING
1658—FIRE IN THE BLOOD

CHARLOTTE LAMB

Guilty Love

Harlequin Books

TORONTO • NEW YORK • LONDON
AMSTERDAM • PARIS • SYDNEY • HAMBURG
STOCKHOLM • ATHENS • TOKYO • MILAN
MADRID • WARSAW • BUDAPEST • AUCKLAND

ISBN 0-373-11706-X

GUILTY LOVE

This edition published by arrangement with Harlequin Enterprises B.V.

Printed in U.S.A.

CHAPTER ONE

'I'M AFRAID I have to ask you to work late again tonight, Mrs York.'

Linzi had been so intent on her work that she hadn't noticed her boss walk into her office, and his deep voice made her jump.

As she looked round at him, her fine silvery hair flicking back from her face, Ritchie Calhoun gave her one of his slow, sardonic smiles. 'Your nerves are in a bad way! I didn't mean to frighten you out of your wits!'

She gave him a wry look. Every time he came into a room he made her jump; he made most of the staff jump. He was that sort of man. Even now she knew him quite well she was never able to relax when he was around. The air seemed to crackle with electricity everywhere he went, he was curt and incisive, and those grey eyes seemed to see right through to the backbone, which was disconcerting. But she could hardly tell him any of that, so she simply said, 'I'm sorry, I was miles away—what did you say, Mr Calhoun?'

'I want you to work late tonight,' he repeated, and Linzi's teeth caught her lower lip, worrying it. Ritchie Calhoun watched the betraying little movement, his eyes shrewd. 'Is that a problem?'

It was always a problem when he wanted her to work late because it upset Barty every time, but when she'd accepted the job Ritchie Calhoun had laid it on the line that she would have to be prepared to work flexible hours, rather than just nine to five, so how could she complain now? After all, he, himself, worked ferociously hard, putting in a twelve-hour day most days. He was usually there when she arrived in the morning and there when she left, unless he was away on some business trip, or working out in the field with one of his construction teams on a difficult project, when, she gathered, he worked even harder for longer hours. It was said that hardbitten construction workers had been known to turn pale at the sight of him bearing down on them if they weren't working hard enough, or had made some stupid mistake. Everyone in the firm admired the man, but they all agreed—it was no easy job working for Ritchie Calhoun.

The good side was that she had plenty of free time on days when he didn't need her and she was earning a lot more money than she ever had before. She and Barty were getting used to having that extra money every month. They had bought new furniture, new linen, curtains, a new dinner set—gradually their little flat was beginning to look the way Linzi wanted it to look and she could never earn this much anywhere else.

That was why Barty didn't force her to give up the job, much as he resented the hours she had to work.

So Linzi shook her head, suppressing a sigh. 'No, no problem. I can work tonight—do you have any idea when I shall get away, though? I have to cook my husband's dinner.'

'Isn't it time he learnt to cook his own?' Ritchie Calhoun drily enquired, his hard mouth twisting. 'Or he could pick up a Chinese takeaway on his way home from work.'

Involuntarily, Linzi laughed at the idea. 'Barty isn't keen on takeaway food, he likes home cooking.' He liked to find her waiting for him when he came home, too, and, if he didn't he sometimes went out again, to a bar to drink his supper. Her laughter died; sadness filled her eyes.

Ritchie Calhoun lounged against her desk, watching her changing expressions. She had a mobile face which gave away too much of what was going on inside her. Her features were delicate: a small, finely moulded nose, high cheekbones, wide eyes the colour of the sea on a sunny day, a soft pink mouth which was generously full and yet sensitive, suggesting to Ritchie a sensual nature you would never suspect from anything else about Linzi York, he thought, eyes narrowing. Linzi looked up and caught him staring, and blushed as if picking up on his secret thoughts.

'And I suppose you do all the housework, too, and wash and iron his clothes for him?' he asked with a faint sarcasm that indicated disapproval.

'It's what Barty's used to; his mother always did those things for him,' she began, then stopped, frowning, angry with herself for sounding as if she was apologising for her husband. Her private life was none of Ritchie Calhoun's business for one thing, and, for another, she loved Barty—it made her happy to take care of him.

'You both work full-time, though,' Ritchie Calhoun pointed out.

'Yes, well...Barty wasn't brought up to look after himself,' she defensively said. 'He was an only child, his mother was middle-aged when he was born, and so thrilled to have a child of her own that I'm afraid she waited on him hand and foot. It made her happy to spoil him.'

'And you've gone on spoiling him?'

She didn't answer that; he saw the flicker of resentment in her face, and her lids came down like shutters over her eyes, to hide her thoughts from him. Ritchie picked up on them all the same: obviously she wasn't happy with all these questions, with the implied criticism of her husband; and of course she had every reason to feel that way. He had no right to interfere or even comment. Their marriage was their business. If she wanted to make a doormat of herself, why should he stop her? Doormats were useful—as he had often found. His mouth twitched with sudden amusement, yet he didn't change the subject. He could never help trying to improve whatever he found and did not approve of.

'Does his mother live near by? Couldn't he have dinner with her?' he suggested, always looking for the practical solution to a problem. That was what made him so good at his business: he knew how to make things work, machinery, money, people.

'His mother's dead,' Linzi said gravely.

Ritchie sobered, pushing back his thick, dark hair with an impatient hand. 'Oh. Sorry to hear that. I've lost both my parents; I know what a gap that makes. Having a family gives you your own support system, doesn't it? Well, then, couldn't he take his father out to dinner?'

'His father died when Barty was a boy.' There was that look of sadness about her again. It turned her blue eyes a strange colour, like slate in the rain, thought Ritchie Calhoun, observing the phenomenon closely. She was endlessly fascinating to watch: never the same two minutes running. Lately he had found himself watching her all the time, and he frowned suddenly, the admission taking him by surprise. He had spent years trying to stop his secretaries getting too interested in him; it would be stupid to fall into the same trap himself.

Yet he was still curious enough to ask, 'When did his mother die?' He moved away from her slightly, however; settled himself on the edge of her desk, his lean body at ease, the long legs crossed and his foot swinging.

'Two years ago.' Linzi was rather perplexed—why was he so interested in Barty's family? She had got used to Ritchie Calhoun's offhand manner at work, his drive and sarcasm. She had never seen him in a mood like this.

'So he has no family now, except you?' Ritchie thought aloud slowly, his eyes thoughtful. Was that why she had gone on spoiling her husband, to comfort him, make up for the loss of his mother?

'No,' she said, her voice low and husky. 'He has nobody but me.'

There was something touching about the way she said it. She had only been working for him for six months and they had never exchanged any personal confidences before. He didn't know why he was asking questions about her private life now; indeed, one part of him protested about the wisdom of showing so much interest in her. Yet he kept on watching her, his grey eyes glimmering, brilliant with curiosity. What was she thinking? What did that look in her eyes mean?

There was something faintly childlike about her, with her long, straight silvery hair and those wide, large-pupilled blue eyes, yet he had begun to sense that there were secrets buried behind her open gaze, and his curiosity, once aroused, wasn't easy to smother. Most of the women he met were so obvious, such simple equations; they didn't hold his interest longer than it took for him to find out what lay behind their smooth, glossy façades.

At first sight he had thought Linzi York was even simpler than usual; she was as calm as milk, as ordinary as bread and butter. It had taken him months to find out his mistake, and even now he didn't really have a clue what she was hiding, only that she was hiding something.

Ritchie Calhoun was determined to get to the bottom of her mystery, however long it took.

'How long have you been married?' he lazily enquired, and she gave him a faintly exasperated glance.

'Four years, ten months.'

It was Ritchie's turn to be startled. 'I'd no idea you'd been married that long!' She didn't look old enough. 'I assumed you had just got married when you joined us.' He remembered their first interview suddenly, with a faint surprise because he saw her differently now.

It had been a cold November morning. She had been wearing a carnation-pink dress and had glowed with warmth in the grey light, yet she had seemed so young. All the same, she had had impressive office skills, good references from her last boss, who had only parted with her because he was moving his firm to another part of the country, and, most important of all, she was married. Ritchie's previous secretary had fallen in love with him, without any encouragement, and had made his life impossible with jealous scenes and weeping in the office. He had had to fire her; it made him shudder just to remember that scene and he hadn't wanted it to happen again, so he had only short-listed married applicants for the job.

He had intended to choose a safe, middle-aged woman, but then Linzi York had walked into the office, and for some inexplicable reason he had found himself offering her the job.

He had rationalised his decision, afterwards, by telling himself that she had a gentle manner, which he knew he would find restful in the office after the hassle he got out on the construction sites; also she was both very capable, and very young—a combination which meant that he would have no difficulty moulding her into the sort of secretary he wanted. And, then, the fact that she was married made her safe to have around.

In fact he admitted to himself now that he really had not known what crazy impulse had made him offer her the job. He still didn't. He was glad he had, though.

All the same, he had encouraged her to keep a distance between them, and he didn't know why he was trying to bridge the gulf now. He would probably regret it tomorrow, but at this moment he found himself intensely curious about her; he wanted to know what sort of life she led, away from the office, what sort of man she had married, and whether the two of them were happy. In the six months they had worked together they had rarely talked about anything but work; he had no idea about her private life.

'What exactly does your husband do?' he asked, and saw her faint bewilderment, the blue gleam of her perfectly shaped eyes as she stared at him, frowning.

Obviously she was surprised by his sudden interest. He would have to be careful she didn't get any wrong ideas and start being afraid he fancied her. He certainly didn't want that.

He lowered his lids but watched her though his black lashes. She was lovely. No question about it. Except that he didn't go for the delicate, faintly ethereal type. All that long, pale hair, the big blue eyes ... he preferred his women sophisticated, experienced, exciting. Yet he kept on watching her, listening to the cool sound of her voice. What would she look like if that dreamy, cool look dissolved? What did she look like when she made love? he wondered, then frowned at his own wandering thoughts.

What on earth was wrong with him, thinking like that? She was married, for one thing, and, for another, the last thing he needed was any more disruption in the office! Stop it! he told himself.

'He's a computer programmer with an electronics firm,' she slowly said. 'Matthews and Cuthlow.'

He knew them and nodded, quite impressed. 'Excellent firm. Computer programming is a job that demands a lot of patience, very complicated stuff usually—

does he like it? Is he good at it? I suppose he must be or he wouldn't be doing it.'

'He's always been clever with machines of any kind.' Actually, Barty found the job boring. He had preferred being a mechanic with a garage that specialised in customising luxury cars and motorbikes. Barty had loved that job, it had broken his heart to give it up, but two years ago he had crashed on his own motorbike and been badly injured. For a while it had looked as if he might die. Linzi had terrible memories of that time. She had been down to hell and back in a few short days; she preferred to forget all about what happened during that week of her life.

Barty had had devoted nursing and good doctors, and he had pulled through, after months of operations and illness, because his body was fit and young and healthy. But the man who came back to her had not been the Barty she had loved and married.

That man had gone forever; perhaps she was the only one in the world who remembered that Barty, now that his mother was dead. He had been full of fun, lighthearted and loving, as much her friend as her lover because they had known each other all their lives. They'd had a few friends, but none of them had ever been very close; and since the accident they hadn't seen much of any of them. They had come round, at first, to visit him, but they were mostly other mechanics, and Barty hadn't wanted to see them, and he'd made that plain.

Barty could no longer stand the strain of hard physical work; it was out of the question for him to go back to his job at the garage, but an old family friend was a top executive in an electronics firm, and had suggested he take up a job as a computer programmer.

Computers had been his hobby for years; Barty had only needed to do a specialist course at a technical college for a year to bring his skills up to the right standard, and the pay was certainly very good. But the programming he was doing was often tedious, and he still suffered from headaches and eye-strain, one of the lasting effects of his accident. Barty would so much rather be doing his old job.

'What are you thinking?' Ritchie Calhoun abruptly broke into her thoughts and Linzi started visibly, gave him one of her wide-eyed looks.

'Oh, just that...I'd better ring my husband right away and warn him I'll be late home. What time do you think I'll get away?'

'No idea,' Ritchie said curtly, turning away with a frown, as if tiring of their conversation. He walked to the door and left without a backward glance, and Linzi watched the back of his dark head with a wry smile.

He was back to normal, was he? She wondered why he had suddenly become so curious, asked all those personal questions. It wasn't at all like him, but Linzi wasn't really interested in Ritchie Calhoun. As the door shut behind him she picked up the phone to ring her husband. Her lips were dry, she moistened them with her tongue-tip, swallowing. Please don't be furious, Barty! she thought as she dialled.

He was, though. 'Tell him no!' he snarled at the other end of the line after she had broken the news to him in a soft, placating voice.

'I can't very well——' she began, and Barty interrupted angrily.

'Oh, yes, you can! Tell him you can't work late. You've been at that office since nine o'clock this morning, for heaven's sake! Nobody should have to work longer than an eight-hour day! You stop working at five-thirty!'

'But, Barty——'

He overrode her, his voice loud and aggressive. 'At five-thirty you just get up and walk out, Linzi! Do you hear me? He can't make you stay. Just tell him you're sorry, but you have to get home to cook your husband's dinner. Tell him to ring me if he wants an argument, and I'll tell him what he can do with his job.'

'I can't do that, Barty,' she said, pleading with him. 'You know I agreed to work flexible hours——'

'You didn't agree to be a slave!' Barty's voice hardened. 'Or did you?'

She tried to talk him out of his mounting temper. 'You know, I don't work that hard, in actual hours. If you average out the time I have off, during the week, and the overtime I work, it comes out more or less right, and the money is good. If I want to keep this job I have to accept odd working hours to fit in with Ritchie——'

'Ritchie now, is it?' Barty's voice snapped like a whip and she tensed, turning paler. This was what she had been afraid of, had been hoping to avoid, arousing his irrational jealousy. 'How long have you been on first-name terms with him?'

'I'm not,' she anxiously denied. 'I was going to use his surname as usual, but you interrupted!'

'Don't try and wriggle out of it! I knew there was something going on, all these late nights, the lame excuses about flexi time and having to fit in with his working hours, not to mention the way you suddenly started earning twice as much as you ever have before— oh, it's obvious what you've been up to, you little——'

'Barty!' she broke out, shaking and holding the phone so tightly that her knuckles showed white. 'Don't!'

His voice sank into bitterness. 'The truth hurts, doesn't it, Lin? I suppose you think you're justified! I can't give you what you need so you feel entitled to get it somewhere else!'

'No,' she whispered, the tears falling down her face. 'That isn't true, Barty, how can you say these things to me? You know I love you, I've always loved you, I haven't changed.'

'But I have!' he snarled. 'Is that what you're saying? It's all my fault for having that crash and not dying afterwards.'

'No, darling! Don't, please, don't. I hate it when you talk like that.'

'You've never liked facing facts, Lin,' he said in a low, harsh voice that was even worse than the angry snarling he had been doing. 'The truth is I shouldn't have gone on living. The way I am, I've no right to life. I'm just a useless piece of machinery that doesn't work any more, I belong on the scrap heap.'

She put a hand over her mouth to stifle the sob wrenched out of her, and desperately tried to think of something to say. If only she was there, with him, she could fling her arms round him and hold on, as she had so many times before, when he suffered like this; she wasn't always able to think of anything to say that he wouldn't shoot down in flames a second later, it was hard to say anything that he hadn't heard before and couldn't dismiss with derisive scorn, but she could always reach him by holding him, convincing him wordlessly that she loved him.

Bleakly, Barty went on, 'At least if I'd died in that crash I could have been recycled—the bits of me that did work could have saved someone else's life! I could have been some use to somebody. My kidneys were fine, my heart works OK, and I have pretty good eyesight, even if my liver isn't up to much any more——'

Her voice trembled as she hurriedly broke in, 'Barty, you know that's not true, you aren't useless, and I'd have wanted to die, too, if you'd died!'

He was silent then for a long moment, and she waited, hardly daring to breathe, praying that she had reached him, calmed him, got to that part buried deep inside him which was still the Barty she had loved all her life.

They had grown up in the same street; he had been literally the boy next door, just a couple of years older than her, and her hero from the minute she could toddle after him calling his name, begging him to wait for her. He had waited, she had caught up with him, they had married very young, and had had such a short time of happiness before tragedy hit them.

Sometimes she thought they had been far too young when they got married, but then if they had waited they might never have married at all. She realised now that

Barty wouldn't have married her after his accident. As it was he had urged her to leave him, to divorce him, but she had refused.

'I love you, Barty,' she whispered into the silence, and heard him sigh.

'It would have been better for you, kid, if I had died, though,' he said flatly, and she let out a shaky sigh of her own, careful not to let him hear it.

'No, darling, it wouldn't, it wouldn't—I need you,' she said quickly, and he almost laughed, the sound a low grunt, bitterly humorous.

'God knows what for!' Then his voice changed, was offhand but softer. 'But thanks, honey. You know I need you. Always have, always will. I got the best of the bargain when we made our wedding vows. I'm afraid you didn't have the same luck. I'm sorry I blew my top, I never mean to, the black dog just bites and . . .'

'I know,' she said gently. 'I know, Barty. It doesn't matter.'

'It damned well does,' he said in another brief spurt of rage. 'I hate myself for what I put you through. Look, I'll work late myself, and eat sandwiches at my bench.'

'Don't give yourself a headache. You know it isn't good for you to spend too long in front of your VDU.'

'Yes, Mummy, and the same to you,' he said, trying to be funny. 'And don't let that bastard Calhoun keep you slaving in front of a hot computer all evening. See you when you do get home. I'll be waiting up with some hot cocoa.'

She blew him a kiss, her mouth tremulous. 'Love you.'

'I don't deserve you, but I do love you,' he said, his voice raw with feeling, then he hung up.

Linzi put the phone down and put her head down on her desk, shaking. That had been a bad moment. For a minute she had thought she wasn't going to be able to stop him going over the edge.

She would have given notice and left this job if she had thought it would make any difference, but by the time she started to work here she'd already known the score. Barty was seeing various specialists, who had all told Linzi the same thing—nothing she did was really triggering Barty's abnormal reactions. It wouldn't help if she stopped working here, except for a day or two. Then he would find something else to blame her for. His dangerous swings of mood were all the result of what had happened to him during the accident, and afterwards. No matter how she tried to please and placate him those mood swings would occur, and during the bad times he would blame her and resent her.

The most she could do to help him was be patient, deal with each moment as it hit her, and if Barty did become violent try to persuade him to take the medication his doctors provided, before he lost control altogether.

So far she had always been able to do that. She hoped to God they never reached that stage. His doctors didn't seem too sure whether he would improve or deteriorate. Sometimes Linzi felt so tired that she no longer cared, but she had to care. Barty needed her to care. Once he had been the strong one, taking care of her. Now it was her turn to take care of Barty.

She lifted her head and sniffed, fumbled for a tissue from the box she kept in one of the desk drawers, wiped her face, her wet eyes, blew her nose.

The door leading into Ritchie Calhoun's office opened suddenly, and he strode in, stopping dead as he saw her face before she could avert it and hide the tearstains.

He frowned across the room at her. 'What's wrong?'

'Nothing, I'm fine. I think I'm starting a cold!' she evaded, tossing the used tissue into her waste-paper basket.

He stood there watching her, unconvinced; his black brows drawn together over those piercing grey eyes of his which saw too clearly.

'What did your husband say when you told him you were working late?' he asked, his tone making it obvious that he had put two and two together very accurately and didn't like the answer. She wished he would mind his own business—he always had, until now. He had never asked so many questions before. Why was he doing it now?

'He's going to get himself a sandwich.'

His mouth twisted. 'Sure he can manage that?'

'Don't be sarcastic!'

He gave her a surprised look and Linzi looked back, bristling, yet surprised by herself. She couldn't remember ever snapping at him before.

Drily Ritchie Calhoun said, 'My mother brought me up to take care of myself, and anyone else who happens to come along! She used to say to me that one day my wife would thank her, but as it turned out I never got around to matrimony before she died, so she never got her thank-you. But I suppose that's why men who expect their wives to wait on them hand and foot annoy me.'

'Was your mother anything like you?' Linzi asked curiously, and he gave her a sudden blindingly vivid smile, which astonished her. This really was a day for firsts! He had never given her a smile like that, any more than he had ever asked so many questions about her private life before.

'I'd like to be able to say yes,' he murmured with wry amusement. 'But to be honest I don't think so. I gather I take after my father's side of the family. My mother was a small woman, with very straight, fine fair hair and...' His voice breaking off, he stared at Linzi fixedly for a moment while she stared back, her blue eyes wide in puzzlement.

'Yes?' she prompted.

'She looked something like you,' Ritchie said slowly. 'It didn't dawn on me until just now, but it's true. She had your build and colouring.'

Maybe that was why had had decided on impulse to pick Linzi for his secretary although his common sense had told him that she was too young and too attractive? he thought. She had fitted some subterranean blueprint in his mind.

Linzi was startled. 'Really?' Rather flattered, she smiled, her small face lighting up, and Ritchie blinked.

'When you smile you look quite different,' he said and she looked up at him, her blue eyes wide open.

He smiled down at her, the hardness of his features softening into charm, and she said slowly, 'So do you.' And then an icy shiver ran down her back.

Ritchie immediately picked up on her abrupt change of mood. 'What is it now?' he asked with a touch of his usual impatience.

'Nothing,' she said huskily. 'Just a ghost walking over my grave.'

CHAPTER TWO

As THE next weeks passed and summer deepened into richness, the gardens full of roses, lavender and the hum of bees, trees in full, green leaf, Linzi's sense of uneasiness deepened, too.

Since the afternoon when Ritchie Calhoun seemed to become curious about her and asked all those questions, their relationship had changed in an indefinable way. He began calling her Linzi, instead of Mrs York, and told her offhandedly, 'You might as well call me Ritchie, by the way.'

That had shaken her. When she first began working for him he'd taken care to let her know that he liked a formal boss-secretary relationship, and that had suited her, as well. It still did.

Working every day with a man was an intimate business; you spent hours together, often alone; you couldn't help getting to know each other well, and there were obvious risks in that, especially if your marriage was unstable and you were lonely or unhappy. She had been relieved that Ritchie Calhoun was so distant.

It seemed to her unwise to drop that formality, but she didn't quite like to argue over it. That might make it seem too important. So she let him call her Linzi, but when she spoke to him she usually still called him Mr

Calhoun, pretending not to notice the dry look he gave her every time she did so.

He was very busy with a project on which he'd been working for weeks. A new road was to be built to bypass a small town half an hour's drive from Leeds. There were other construction companies competing for the contract but Ritchie felt sure he had the edge on them because it was the sort of job his firm had often handled in the past and he already had a lot of the machinery required, and a very good workforce, so he could keep his estimate low without taking the risk of cutting dangerous corners on the price of materials. If his firm was awarded the contract it would fit in very usefully with other work they had to complete during that period. It would mean, in fact, that he wouldn't have to lay off any of the casual workers he hired for specific jobs, and Ritchie Calhoun was the sort of employer who liked to be able to offer his employees job stability.

He might be a tough boss who insisted things were done his way, but he was popular with his men. He got his hands dirty, too; he thought nothing of working side by side with them, drinking in the pub with them, and knew all their first names. He could do any job on site and had forgotten more about building than most of them had yet learned. They thought he was a great guy and would work themselves to a standstill for him.

Linzi had learnt to respect, him, too, which was another reason why she didn't want to change jobs, if she could help it.

July was very hot; nobody wanted to work much, everyone wore as little as possible, and had deep tans;

dogs lay about, panting; beaches were crammed with people. Linzi had to work, though. She managed to get time off to go swimming in the local pool some days, but she had to work late every evening for a week, and Barty bitterly resented it.

On the Friday evening Ritchie finally finished the long presentation he had been dictating to her for hours, which she keyed in to the computer while he walked about behind her talking. He came to a halt behind her, massaging the back of his neck.

'God, I'm tired! That's it, Linzi. You might as well get off home. You can print that out on Monday morning.' Then he looked at the clock. 'Is it that late? And you haven't had a bite to eat since lunchtime? Why didn't you say something? We could have had sandwiches brought in.'

'Never mind, I'll cook myself something when I get home.' She had been sitting in one position for so long that when she got up cramp knotted her leg muscles and she staggered slightly.

'Are you OK?' Ritchie put an arm round her and for a second she leaned on him and was suddenly aware of his strength: it was like leaning on a rock. She felt intolerably weary at that instant; she wanted to put all her weight on him, cling, like ivy. She hadn't been able to lean on anyone else for so long. She had had to be the strong one in her marriage ever since Barty's accident. Oh, she'd told herself she didn't need to lean; she could stand alone, could cope with whatever life threw at her, and no doubt she had this strange yearning only because she was exhausted and at the end of her tether.

It didn't mean any more than that, yet she was stricken, shamed by her fleeting weakness. Face burning, she stumbled away from him.

'Sorry...I'm fine,' she lied and was conscious of his sardonic, watchful gaze.

'You don't look it. You're as white as a ghost. I've never seen you look so frail. I could kick myself for working you so hard, it was damned thoughtless of me. I'm sorry, Linzi—why don't we go somewhere and have dinner, a bottle of wine to put some colour back in your face?'

'No!' she broke out wildly, and saw his brows rise at her tone. She bit her lip. 'I...thanks, but I must get home.'

'What are you scared of, Linzi?' he drily asked. 'That I'll make a pass at you? I won't, I assure you. I don't make passes at married women. That isn't my style. You'll be quite safe with me.'

She couldn't even meet his eyes. 'No, of course not, that isn't...I just have to get home,' she stammered. 'My husband will be worried about me.'

He didn't argue any more; just followed her out to the car park and watched her climb into her red Ford Sierra.

'I'll be working out of the office on Monday morning, don't forget,' he told her before she drove away, and she nodded. 'Have a restful weekend,' he added.

When she got home Barty was out. He didn't get back until midnight and by then Linzi was asleep. She had tried to stay awake but her body was too weary. She woke up when Barty fell over something in the sitting-room of their small flat. The crash, followed by swearing, shocked her awake; she sat up just as the bedroom door opened and the light blazed on, blinding her.

'Oh, there you are, you little tramp!' Barty muttered thickly, glaring at her across the room. She could see at once that he had been drinking heavily; he was unsteady on his feet, his face flushed and blurred with drink, his eyes bloodshot.

Alarm leapt up inside her; she tensed, very pale. When he was this drunk he sometimes became violent and started hitting her. Next day he was always horrified, would cry and beg her to forgive him, and she always did.

You couldn't stop loving someone because they were going through a very bad period, and she had loved Barty for as long as she could remember. They had both been through so much together; the bonds of pain bound them as strongly as the bonds of passionate love had done long ago.

'I'm sorry I was late again, Barty,' she said quietly, hoping to placate him. 'But it won't be so bad next week because we won't be quite so busy. We've been preparing a presentation for this new contract...'

His lip curled as he stared at her. 'Don't give me that! I know what you've been doing with him. I thought this time you were staying with him all night—that's the next step, isn't it? You'll want to spend all night with him, lovers always do. Or has he got a wife who might object?'

Linzi was too tired to cry. Wearily she said, 'Don't start that again, Barty. How many times do I have to tell you there's nothing personal between me and Ritchie Calhoun?'

Barty lurched towards her. 'Liar!'

'Stop it, Barty!'

He leaned over her, swaying on his feet. His brown hair was dishevelled, he had lost his tie, and his shirt was open. He still looked so young, she thought, watching him unhappily—there was a lot of the boy left in him. He was too thin, painfully thin, although there was a puffiness around the jaw and eyes that came from drinking, his skin was always sallow and his hazel-brown eyes had heavy shadows under them, but she could still trace the old Barty there.

'I'm not putting up with it any more!' he snarled at her. 'You're giving him notice on Monday. Do you hear? You're leaving that job, or leaving me—take your pick!'

Warily she said, 'We'll talk about it in the morning.'

'We'll talk about it now!'

Linzi could see there was no arguing with him in this state, so she slid out of the bed and picked up her robe from the nearby chair.

'Where do you think you're going?' Barty demanded.

'To sleep on the couch,' she said, suddenly angry.

'Oh, no, you don't!' Barty took hold of her by her long, silky hair, and shook her, making tears start into her eyes.

'Barty, you're hurting me!' she cried out, and he suddenly threw her away from him. She fell heavily across the bed. The edge of the headboard hit her cheekbone and she gave a cry of pain, stumbling up, a hand to her face.

'Why don't you just admit it?' Barty shouted. 'He's your lover, isn't he? Isn't he?'

'No, Barty!' she moaned, her voice rising higher. 'No, no, no!'

'Yes,' he screamed, and hit her hard. She was too shocked to cry. She stumbled backwards again, fell on to the bed, and before she could scramble up again Barty threw himself on top of her, wrenching his clothes off while he held her down with the weight of his body.

'You're my wife!' he muttered hoarsely. He hadn't tried to make love to her for many months; there had been a time when he'd kept trying, growing more and more humiliated, more and more frustrated. Linzi had tried desperately too, knowing that, physically, it was possible. His doctors had told her that firmly. He would never now be able to father a child, but that didn't mean he couldn't make love. The blockage was in his mind— not in his body. She didn't know if they were right or not; but in the end Barty had given up trying. His ego couldn't take the constant failures.

But now his desire was spurred by jealousy and rage; Linzi shuddered with misery as he tried again, his face set, flushed, more with hatred and a drive to impose his possession of her, she felt, than passion. She felt no desire for him; she hadn't for a long time, and although she didn't resist him she couldn't hide her lack of a response. All she felt for Barty now was a weary compassion and a tenderness which was mostly old affection and kindness.

If Barty wanted her body, she would let him have it, for old times' sake, because she was his wife and he had been her best friend all her life. But it was useless, he couldn't do it. Angrily, more and more desperately, he tried—then he slackened and lay still, trembling like a beaten animal on top of her, before rolling off and lying on his face, his body racked by dry sobs.

Linzi put her arms around him and tried to comfort him, wordlessly murmuring, but he pushed her away.

'Leave me alone! It's all your fault. How can I make love to a woman who doesn't want me? Do you think I don't know you don't? Do you think I can't feel you shrinking away from me? You despise me because I can't give you a baby, I'm not a real man...'

'No, Barty, no, darling,' she assured him, stroking his hair, and pulled him back towards her, holding him tightly, cuddling him against her like a frightened child. 'I love you, I've never despised you, and it doesn't matter about babies, we can always adopt one. Why don't we do that? We're young, we should be able to adopt...'

There was a touch of hope in her voice: if they could have a child maybe this would finally end, this nightmare in which they had been lost for two years? They would be a real family again, love would come back, and Barty would be his old self.

But he lifted his head and glowered at her. 'I don't want someone else's baby! I want my own! The one we were going to have when——'

'Don't!' she cried out in agony, as if he had knifed her to the heart. 'Don't talk about that.'

She never had, since the day Barty crashed and the news made his mother collapse with a heart attack and die a day later, just hours before Linzi lost the baby she had been carrying. They had all been in the same hospital that week—Barty in a coma, knowing nothing of what was happening to the two women he loved; his mother dying in the heart ward with Linzi at her bedside when she did so, and later that very day Linzi herself going into premature labour and losing her baby. Linzi had discovered how it felt to be in hell that week.

'You see?' Barty said bitterly. 'You can't even talk about it! That's why you don't love me any more. Your great dream was to have children, a family of your own—do you think I don't remember how happy you were when you discovered you were going to have our baby? It was all going to come true for us, wasn't it? And then I crashed and Mum died and you lost the baby, and ever since then you've hated me.'

'I've never hated you, Barty, I couldn't do that, I love you, this is all in your own mind...and Ritchie Calhoun, too, none of that is true, there's nothing between me and him.'

'Then why won't you give that job up?' he muttered, and Linzi gave a long, weary sigh.

'Yes. We can't go on like this, Barty—I see that. I'll resign on Monday, and get another job.' She didn't want to do it, but tonight had been the worst so far. She knew she couldn't bear much more. She was only human and she was being pushed to her limit. Barty's outbursts were growing more violent; she would have to talk to his specialist. It was very worrying.

Barty subsided. 'Right...right...you do that,' he said, and fell asleep shortly afterwards, suddenly, leaving Linzi beside him, wide awake and dark-eyed. She didn't get back to sleep for hours.

When she woke up, it was broad daylight and she was alone in the bed. For a second she couldn't remember what had happened the night before. She looked at the clock in alarm—had she overslept? Was she going to be late for work? It was nearly ten o'clock and she jumped up, only to realise it was Saturday and she didn't have to work.

She heard noises in the kitchen, and began to remember last night, her colour draining away, her eyes darkening. She was going to have to leave her job. She had promised Barty, and she would have to keep her word.

Ritchie wasn't going to be pleased; it wasn't going to be easy telling him. Well, once she had she would never see him again, so what did it matter what he thought? But it did. Her lip trembled and she put a hand to her mouth. She didn't want to go. She would miss him...

Stop that! she angrily told herself. You have no right to miss him—you're Barty's wife and he needs you. Forget Ritchie Calhoun, he's no concern of yours. If you are starting to have feelings about him it's just as well you're giving up the job.

A moment later Barty came in, wearing a black and red towelling robe under which he was naked, carrying a tray of tea and toast.

She sat up, pushing back her dishevelled silvery hair, and Barty halted, staring at her. His face stiffened, went white, his eyes ringed with puffy shadow.

'Oh, Linzi, what have I done to you?' he whispered. 'Your poor little face...'

She looked at him uncertainly, not quite sure how his mood would swing.

He carried the tea and toast over to the bedside table, put the tray down and sat beside her, dropping his head into his hands. 'I didn't even remember this morning. Can you believe that? I didn't even remember doing anything to you.'

She could believe it. It wasn't the first time he had blotted out the events of the night before.

He slowly lifted his head. 'I am sorry, Linzi, bitterly sorry... I'll try, I'll really try, not to let anything like this happen again.' His hazel eyes seemed so sincere; dark with regret and sadness.

She nodded, her mouth quivering.

Leaning over, he kissed her bruised cheekbone lingeringly. 'I won't ask you to forgive me, I know I don't deserve it... but just say you know I never meant to hurt you like that? You know I love you, don't you, Linzi?' There was despair in his eyes. 'You won't leave me, will you?'

You didn't walk out on someone you had loved just because fate had played a dirty trick on them. It wasn't Barty's fault that he was no longer the man she had married; he hadn't asked to be crippled like this, to suffer these black moods, burst out in violent rage without warning. She knew he loved her.

'I won't go,' she promised.

'I'll never drink like that again, never,' he said, and she wished she could believe him. Oh, he meant it, right now, at this minute—he had meant it many times before when he made this same promise, although never before had he been so violent.

At least he was sober enough to listen now, so she repeated, 'Barty, there is nothing going on between me and Ritchie Calhoun, I swear that to you—but, all the same, I will give notice on Monday.'

'No, don't,' he said, and she looked at him in disbelief, her eyes wide. 'I believe you, Linzi, of course there's nothing going on between you and your boss. It's just my crazy jealousy, but I'm going to be different from now on. I won't ever let that happen again.'

When she saw herself in the mirror in the bathroom later she was shocked. Her face was badly bruised, along the cheekbone, above the eye, around the mouth—she looked terrible. Last night, she hadn't realised just how badly Barty had beaten her. No wonder he had looked shaken when he came in with the tea and toast.

Maybe it would finally snap him out of this dangerous cycle of mood swings? Linzi closed her eyes and prayed. Oh, please, let him stop drinking, let him be the Barty I knew and loved and married. Take away this dangerous stranger, who sometimes seems to hate me; and give me back my love.

When she went into work the following Monday everyone stared. 'Linzi, your face! What on earth happened?'

She had a story ready. 'I tripped coming downstairs, I was lucky not to break any bones.'

She sounded so casual, laughing, that they all seemed to believe her. Ritchie Calhoun wasn't there, he was

working out of the office that morning, but he walked
in later, just before she was due to leave for home.

She had forgotten her bruises and looked up in surprise as her office door opened and he appeared.

He was smiling, but the smile died as he saw her face.
'Good God!' he broke out, his brows dragging together.

She remembered then, and put a defensive hand up
to her cheek, bit her lip. 'Oh...I...' For a second she
couldn't remember the lie she had invented for everyone
else who had asked. Stammering, she finally managed
to say, 'I fell downstairs. It isn't as bad as it looks.'

Ritchie strode over to her desk and she flinched as if
he might hit her, and saw the flash of his grey eyes as
he observed the betraying little movement.

'Well, it looks terrible!' he said and pushed her hand
down, touching her cheek with his own hand.

She began to tremble, her body pulsating fiercely. His
skin was cool against her hot face; he gently touched
the bruise and seemed to draw the pain out of it, then
his fingertips slid down her cheek to explore her bruised
and swollen mouth.

She drew a long, deep, shaky breath. He touched her
so lightly, like the brush of a moth in the night; her skin
tingled afterwards. It was hard to believe that so tough
a man could be so gentle.

'Have you seen a doctor?' Ritchie brusquely demanded, as if accusing her of something, and she was
snapped out of her trance-like mood.

'No, of course not, it isn't that serious.'

'I think it is,' he snapped.

'It happened two days ago! If I had anything seriously wrong with me I'd have noticed by now!'

'Two days ago?' he repeated. 'On Friday night?'

'Yes,' she said, wishing he wouldn't stare. It was like being under a searchlight; there was nowhere for her to hide, no way of disguising from him what she was feeling.

'When you got home, after we worked late?'

The question hit her like a bolt from the blue and she went white then red as she realised he had guessed what had really happened.

She invented rapidly, feverishly. 'On the way home,' she said. 'As I got out of the car. I tripped and hit my head on a wall.'

Drily he reminded her, 'You said you fell over coming downstairs—which was it?'

'What is this? An interrogation?' she threw back at him resentfully.

He sat down on the edge of her desk and watched her closely. 'Isn't it time you talked about it, Linzi? What's going on? And don't insult my intelligence by telling me nothing is...we both know that isn't true. You aren't happy, something is very wrong with your marriage, and now you start coming in to work with bruises on your face? It would help to talk about it, you know.'

'No, it wouldn't,' she said. 'It wouldn't help at all. Please drop the subject, Mr Calhoun. My private life is none of your business.'

'Maybe I'm making it my business!' he retorted, his face grim.

'In that case I'll have to resign,' she said in a quiet, cool tone.

The grey eyes flashed; for a second she was afraid he wasn't going to accept the warning, but then he got up and walked away without another word.

That evening, when she got home, Barty told her that his firm were sending him on a training course to Manchester for a week, and the stimulation of a break in his routine was good for him. He was more cheerful for the rest of the week. He left on Sunday night and Linzi slept well for the first time in months.

The next few days were the most peaceful Linzi had had since the accident. She felt oddly younger, lighter, a sense of freedom in everything she did while she didn't have to look over her shoulder all the time in case Barty should suddenly turn nasty. It helped that Ritchie was out of the office, too, that week, working on the site of his latest project.

On the Thursday, however, a very hot day in late July, she answered the phone to hear Ritchie's voice, 'Linzi, would you check my office and see if I've left my black briefcase there? I'll hang on, but hurry.'

She laid the phone down and hurried into his adjoining office. She knew the briefcase he meant; he carried it everywhere when he was touring his sites or having a business meeting out of the office. It wasn't on his desk or on the floor, she she checked the wall cupboard where he kept his large maps, site plans, tripods and cameras, and other construction impedimenta, and that was where she found the briefcase, open as if he had been filling it with maps and forgotten to take it with him.

She ran back to the phone with it and told Ritchie, who groaned. 'Damnation take it! Well, I have to have it, and it would take up too much time for me to come back—you'll have to bring it to me. You have your own car, don't you, Linzi?'

'Yes, but what about the office?'

'Get Petal in to man the phones while you're gone, then drive out here, with the briefcase. I'm at the Green Man roundabout, that's Junction 43 off the motorway—take the Hillheath road; that brings you straight here. I'm here with Ted; he's going to fly me over the course of the new road in the afternoon, in the helicopter, but I must have those air maps here or Ted and I will just be wasting our time. You can get here by one if you leave straight away.'

He hung up and she did, too, sighing. She had a pile of work to do and she knew Petal wouldn't be up to coping with any of it.

She turned off her computer and put the confidential documents into a filing cabinet, which she locked, then, picking up the briefcase, she went into an office across the hallway where personnel matters were handled. There was a staff of three, but this morning only one of them was visible; the others were no doubt visiting other offices.

Petal was the one left; she was making coffee while she printed out a sheaf of letters to construction staff on some union matter. Petal ran the personnel office daily routine. She was a large woman in her forties; a

brunette who wore too much rouge and had a passion
for pink frilly blouses. Her real name was Rose, but she
thought it was old-fashioned, and, since her husband,
a Yorkshireman with a droll sense of humour, always
called her Petal, everyone else did too. 'Hi, Linzi—want
a cup of coffee?' she cheerfully asked when Linzi came
into the room. 'I've got your favourite chocolate biscuits today.'

'I haven't got time,' Linzi regretfully said, and explained that Petal was going to be left in charge of the
phones in Ritchie Calhoun's office.

'Oh, glory!' Petal looked aghast. She was helpful and
willing, but not exactly quick-witted, and Ritchie
Calhoun made her nervous. He expected too much.
'Must I? I'm bound to get into a muddle, and then he'll
tear me limb from limb,' she wailed. 'Couldn't someone
else take over?'

'Sorry, Petal,' Linzi said, shaking her head. There were
younger girls working in other offices, but Ritchie
Calhoun had specified Petal, so that was that.

'When will you be back?'

'I've no idea, at least a couple of hours, I expect. Just
take messages and say I'll ring back anyone who needs
an urgent response.'

Ten minutes later she was heading towards the
motorway, Ritchie's briefcase locked safely in the boot
of her car. She was glad to be out of the office: it was
such a hot day that it was hard to work indoors. She
drove with her window wide open and a cooling breeze
blowing her silvery hair around her sunflushed face.

There was quite a bit of traffic, so it took her longer to reach the Green Man roundabout than she had expected.

She only drew into the car park of the public house at ten past one and there was no sign of Ritchie, although she spotted his red Jaguar parked near by. He was presumably in the restaurant, at the back of the building, eating his lunch with Ted, the pilot of the company helicopter.

Linzi found the cloakroom first, looked at herself ruefully in the mirror, and set about making herself look more presentable. She was wearing a neat white shirt and straight navy skirt, her usual office uniform.

So she added a smart red blazer with small gold buttons, which she had only bought the day before but which immediately gave a touch of class to the very ordinary skirt and top. Then she ran a comb through her windblown hair, powdered her nose, put on tiny gold earrings which matched the buttons in her blazer, and clipped a gold chain round her throat.

Two minutes later she paused in the doorway of the restaurant, looking around the room. She spotted Ritchie immediately, seated facing her, at a discreet table in an alcove. He saw her, at the same time, and lifted an imperative hand, beckoning her.

She walked over to join the two men, very conscious of Ritchie Calhoun's hard grey eyes watching her all the way. He was wearing his site working gear—hard-wearing blue jeans, an open-necked plaid shirt, strong boots. He looked even tougher dressed like that: more obviously a powerful man—with a lot of muscle and very fit—

than he ever looked in a suit with a shirt and tie. He could have been any one of his workers, until you looked into his eyes and saw the cold glint of intelligence there, the habit of authority, the look of a man who knew that when he gave an order other men jumped to obey it.

Linzi felt a shudder ripple through her from head to foot. He was a very disturbing man. She wished she weren't so aware of him, but he radiated a powerful male sexuality that was hard to ignore. Hard for her, anyway. Her mouth had gone dry and there was a terrifying heat inside her.

Ted Hobson gave her a broad grin. 'Hello, Linzi, love.' He was a small, wiry man in his thirties, with deft hands, shrewd eyes and thick brown hair.

She had met him in the office several times; he flew Ritchie backwards and forwards, from site to site, if they were too far apart for a car journey to be practicable. She managed a shy smile.

'Hello, Ted. How's Megan?'

His eyes lit up. 'Fine, thanks; the new baby's due any day now and we're hoping it will be a girl. Megan won't let the hospital tell her whether it is or not—she'd rather wait and find out the usual way. I think she's afraid to let them tell her, in case it's not a girl.'

'But Megan will love it whatever it is!' smiled Linzi, and Ted grinned, nodding.

'Oh, aye. Once it's here she'll be happy whatever it is. My Megan is crazy about babies.'

Megan and Ted had invited Linzi and Barty to a party soon after Linzi began working for the company. It had been fun until Barty had had one drink too many, and

turned obstreperous when Linzi tried to persuade him
to go home with her. He snarled, pushed her roughly
away, and she had been very embarrassed, in front of a
room full of people from work. Megan had been wonderful. A large, tranquil woman with glossy brown hair
and a warm smile, she had appeared beside them, put
an arm around Barty and coaxed, 'Will you dance with
me, Barty?'

He had blinked at her owlishly and stuttered, 'Sure,
Meg...Meg...an! I'd love to d...dance with you.'

She had whirled him round the room, aiming for the
door, and Barty had clung on to her, his head only too
obviously going round too. Linzi had followed, avoiding
the amused or sympathetic glances she was getting from
other guests. Outside in the hall Barty was sitting on the
bottom of the stairs, leaning against the wall, his eyes
glazed.

'Here's Linzi to take you home,' Megan said softly.
'Up we come, there's a good boy.'

Together they had got him to his feet and steered him
out of the house and into the car.

'Can you manage at the other end? Would you like
me to come home with you?' Megan had asked her, and
Linzi had shaken her head, very flushed.

'No, I'll manage, but thanks, he doesn't usually drink
so much...'

The lie had stuck in her throat and she had repeated
huskily, 'But thanks, Megan, and I'm sorry we spoiled
your party.'

'You didn't, don't be silly. These things happen at
parties—we understand, forget the whole thing. Now,

you drive carefully.' She had looked into the car and laughed. 'Look, he's sleeping like a baby. By the time you get home he'll be himself again.'

Ever since that night, Linzi had thought of Megan as a friend, and they had met for lunch several times when Ted was flying Ritchie Calhoun to some far-flung corner of Britain.

Megan and Ted had three sons, all at school now. The baby she was expecting would, she said, be her last child and if she didn't want a little girl so badly she wouldn't have wanted another child at all, not that she didn't love her boys.

She was a warm and loving mother and she and Ted were clearly very happy together. Linzi envied Megan; the older woman had everything she wanted and would probably never have now.

Ritchie took the briefcase from her and gestured to a third chair placed at the table. 'Sit down and have some lunch. We haven't ordered yet.'

She hesitated. 'Shouldn't I get back to the office?'

'Sit down and don't argue!'

Ted winked at her. Linzi sat down and picked up the menu just as the waiter came over to the table. The men immediately began ordering their lunch; they both wanted melon followed by steak. Linzi ordered melon too, and a prawn and cottage cheese salad.

'No wine for me,' Ritchie said, shaking his head at the wine-list he was offered. 'What would you like to drink, Linzi?'

She asked for a fizzy mineral water and the waiter left. Ted grinned at her.

'I have to watch what I drink when I'm flying, especially on a day as hot as this! Aren't you hot in that jacket, Linzi, love?'

'No, I'm fine...'

'Yes, take it off,' Ritchie said in his curt, determined way, and he got up and came behind her. 'All this hair!' he added wryly. 'Doesn't it get in the way?' and he pushed it aside.

Heat rushed up Linzi's face as she felt his fingertips brush the nape of her neck. Her breathing seemed to stop. She began to shake. It was all over in a flash; he removed her jacket in one deft movement and hung it neatly over the back of her chair, then he went back to his own chair and sat down again. Their eyes met across the table. He was as flushed as she was and his eyes looked dark, smouldering like coals.

'Doesn't that feel better?' asked Ted, seeming oblivious to the atmosphere between them.

Linzi nodded, her pulses drumming. The waiter arrived with her drink and the melon they had all ordered. It was very prettily arranged, thinly sliced, in a fan, with raspberries scattered around it, one slice of star fruit at the upper edge.

'Isn't that pretty?' Linzi said huskily.

'I don't like my food pretty,' Ted complained. 'It makes me wonder if I'm supposed to eat it or frame it and hang it on the wall!'

Linzi pretended to laugh. She lowered her eyes to her plate, took a raspberry to pop into her mouth and under cover of eating it gave Ritchie a nervous, secret, sideways, look through her lashes. Had he noticed what just happened to her? She'd want to die if he had; oh, God, how humiliating. And she couldn't even explain, she couldn't tell him that it didn't mean anything, it wasn't personal, any man might have got the same reaction, that drumming pulse, the drowning sensuality which came from long-frustrated need. The heat grew in her face. Well, not any man! she hastily contradicted. It had never happened with any man before, after all; this was the first time in years she had felt that flashpoint of desire.

Why should it have come just now while Ritchie Calhoun was touching her? She didn't even like him! He disturbed her, made her jumpy.

He had felt something, too—she was sure of that. Her intuition had picked up on the vibrations inside him, she had known when she looked into those darkened eyes of his. He had felt something . . .

Desire, she thought—why pretend you don't know he felt it too? It was there between them, throbbing like a dynamo. A desire like nothing she had ever felt in her life before.

You're married! she fiercely reminded herself, digging her nails into her palms. Whatever Barty has done to you, you are still his wife, and he loves you even when he acts as if he hates you. The pain made it easier to snap out of her mood.

Ritchie was frowning over a map he had got out of his briefcase. He hadn't touched his food yet. A heavy lock of black hair fell forward over his eyes, and he brushed it impatiently back with one lean, tanned hand.

Linzi looked away, swallowing convulsively. She must stop this! Stop noticing everything he does! she told herself angrily.

Oh, Barty, what has happened to us? she thought in a swell of agony, remembering how passionately they had once made love. How merciful that you could never guess the future, that it was veiled from sight until it hit you.

She pushed her thin slices of melon around the plate, forced herself to eat, the cool fruit sliding down her parched throat, the perfect food for a day as hot as this one. Maybe it was the weather that was making her act so strangely, so unlike herself?

Ritchie began talking to Ted, flung the open map across the table between them, pointing, then picked up his fork and ate his own melon while Ted was studying the map.

'Have you been up in a chopper yet?' Ted asked her, and Linzi shook her head. 'Well, come with us today,' he suggested.

'Good idea,' Ritchie said. 'It's time you realised how vital the air dimension is to planning, Linzi. Seeing a site on a map or even on the ground you don't get the full picture, but fly over it and you realise how much you miss until you've seen it from the air.'

'I ought to get back to the office,' she demurred.

'Nonsense. Petal can hold the fort for an afternoon.'

The waiter brought their second course; Linzi ate some of her salad, trying to think of a way out of going up in the helicopter with them, but Ritchie was like a bulldozer once he had made up his mind. He wouldn't be stopped or turned aside.

Half an hour later Linzi found herself crossing a mown field towards the waiting helicopter.

'Up you get!' Ritchie said, seizing her waist and lifting her up. Ted showed her how to belt herself into her seat, and gave her headphones to wear, to shut out the noise. Ritchie clambered in beside them, and the door closed. Linzi stared up at the whirling blades, her eyes blurred by the speed at which they went round. The machine began to lift and she looked down to see their black shadow flying across the ground below.

Ritchie tapped her shoulder, gesticulated downwards, mouthed, 'Along this ridge, the line of poplars . . . that's the route.'

The landscape flowed beneath them; fields, hills, trees in a fascinating pattern of light and shade, colour and contour. Linzi could have flown over it forever. She had never been so absorbed. Ritchie spread the map out on her lap, traced their route with his hand; she looked from the map to the landscape, connecting them, understanding their relationship, and deeply excited.

'It's wonderful!' she said, looking up into Ritchie's face with glowing blue eyes, and he smiled at her, nodding.

At that instant the engine note changed, missed a beat, began to make a choking sound. Ritchie stiffened, looking at Ted. Ted was staring at the instruments on the panel, his hands moving, making some sort of checks. Linzi sat very still, realising something was wrong.

'What is it, Ted?' Ritchie quietly asked.

Ted gave him a sideways look. 'I think we'd better put down. That field right below us will do, it's very flat. Hold on to your hats, sit still and don't touch anything.'

Their rate of descent was faster than their rate of ascent had been; they were coming down in strange, irregular circles, dipping sideways.

We're going to crash, Linzi realised.

'Listen, keep your seatbelt on until we...we're down...' Ritchie hurriedly told her. 'But the minute we are down undo the belt, jump out and run...don't wait for anyone else...'

They were probably all going to be killed, that was what he meant, but he was afraid to tell her the truth in case she panicked and went into hysterics.

She gave him a calm smile. 'OK.'

Ritchie looked at her oddly, frowning. 'You understand?'

'Yes.' She wasn't afraid of dying. Life wasn't such a wonderful experience. Flying over the green and gold landscape, she had experienced a beauty which remained inside her now and made it somehow easier to contemplate death. When she thought of the pain and ugliness her life sometimes held, death seemed quite an attractive alternative.

Ritchie made a sound like a groan. 'You're amazing. Cool as a cucumber; are you for real?'

'Is anything?' she said, and even laughed.

'Brace yourselves,' Ted said. 'Any second now.'

And then the helicopter hit the ground and for a moment Linzi didn't know what was happening. The machine crashed, shuddered, bounced, whirled and skidded, while she and the two men were thrown this way and that, their bodies helpless to resist. The chopper ended up in a hedge, at an angle which made the sky dip crazily above them.

'Out!' Ritchie shouted; his hands fumbled with her seatbelt and she helped him undo it. A few seconds later, he pushed her out of the door and she half slid, half fell to the ground. They had landed in a field of wheat, trampling the tall golden stems.

'Get up and run!' Ritchie shouted as he leapt out after her, with Ted not far behind, and she automatically obeyed.

'Why are we running?' she asked breathlessly, but neither of the men answered. They didn't need to. A moment later there was a great crash and a roar as the chopper blew up.

The wind from the explosion came after them in a wave of heat which knocked Linzi off her feet. She fell on her face in the wheat: the smell of it made her nostrils quiver; the rasp of the stalks on her skin was an intensely felt experience.

'Linzi! Are you OK?' Ritchie asked with harsh anxiety as he knelt beside her and lifted her in his arms.

She looked up at him, her lips curving in a smile of happiness; she had never felt so intensely alive before, nor so conscious of how beautiful the world was.

Ritchie stared into her blue eyes, his face taut and pale. 'Oh, God, Linzi, I was afraid you might be dead, I was terrified,' he whispered, and then his mouth was on hers, compelling, hot, passionate.

It was like being hit by lightning. One minute she was laughing, happy to be alive; the next she was burning with a response to his kiss which shook her to her very depths. Her mouth quivered wildly for an instant, her eyes closing, then she began to kiss him back with mounting hunger, trembling from head to foot in his arms.

As suddenly as the storm began, it ended. Breathing thickly, darkly flushed, Ritchie broke off the kiss, took a long, ragged breath and pulled her to her feet.

She was appalled. She couldn't meet his eyes; she didn't know how to handle the moment and hastily turned away only to stop dead, her eyes huge and shocked. Behind her Ritchie had just seen what she was staring at, too. She heard the harsh intake of his breath.

Ted lay on his face unmoving, several feet away.

CHAPTER THREE

RITCHIE ran over and knelt beside Ted, saying his name. 'Ted...Ted, are you OK?' He gently turned him over; Linzi heard his intake of breath. She was shocked, herself, to see the blood running down Ted's face. It hadn't been there when they first climbed out of the helicopter; Ted had had visible bruises, no doubt caused by their crash landing, when they were all thrown around violently before the machine finally shuddered to a stop, but there had been no blood.

'He's been hit by something—a fragment of metal from the chopper, maybe?' Ritchie said slowly. 'When it blew, it must have sprayed the air with something like shrapnel.'

She looked round in horror at the burning helicopter; the flames were reaching up towards the sky and had set the field of wheat on fire.

'We've all got to get out of here!' she gasped, and Ritchie looked round, followed the direction of her pointing finger, anxiety deepening in his eyes as he realised what she meant.

'I don't think it's safe to move Ted!' he muttered, putting a long, brown index finger against Ted's neck, searching for a pulse.

'What choice do we have?' Linzi was watching the fire; the wheat was tinder-dry and burned fiercely, and there was something terrifying in the speed with which the fire spread. The smell of burning filled the air; a column of black smoke climbed upwards.

'Someone's bound to see that,' Ritchie thought aloud. 'Ted's heart sounds fine, but we've got to get him to a doctor fast.' He stood up, frowning, then suddenly swore angrily, making Linzi jump. He gave her a scowling look. 'Sorry, I don't usually swear like that in front of women, but I've just realised, the maps were all in the chopper, so I can't work out exactly where we are. I had a good look around as we were coming down; there's a main road across a couple of fields and I spotted a village some miles away but heaven knows where the nearest hospital is!' He ran a hand despairingly through his dark hair. 'Oh, why did this have to happen to us?'

The crackling, roaring sound of the fire was making Linzi very nervous. 'We must get out of here, Ritchie!'

He nodded, then went up to the hedge and peered over it, gave a little grunt. 'That's lucky! There's a ditch here on this side of the hedge, half full of water. That should act as a natural fire break, so long as sparks don't fly across the hedge. At least it will delay the spread of the fire.' He turned to look at the burning helicopter. 'The fire's moving away from us, look—watch the way the wheat bends, that means that whatever breeze there is is blowing in that direction. Right, I'll take Ted's shoulders, you take his feet. We'll carry him into the next field, and then I'll have to try to get help. But we can't leave Ted alone.'

'No, of course not, I'll stay with him,' she said, gripping Ted's feet and watching as Ritchie lifted him by the shoulders.

'Sure you won't be scared?'

'Sure.'

His eyes searched her face again. She gave him a faint smile, nodding. 'Don't worry about me, I'll cope.'

Ritchie gave her a brief, wry smile. 'I'm sure you will. OK, but listen, if he recovers consciousness, try to keep him awake, talk to him, tell him where I've gone, say anything to grab his attention and keep him from passing out again.'

'I understand,' she said, moving carefully so as not to jolt Ted too much as she manipulated him through the open gate.

Ritchie kicked the gate shut behind them. 'We'll carry him as far as possible around this field. Look, Linzi, it would be better if you went and I stayed with Ted, then at least I could carry him over my shoulder to the road.'

She looked back. 'The fire is still moving away from us, though!'

Ritchie frowned. 'OK.' They paused, breathing heavily. Ritchie lowered Ted to the ground. 'You should be fine here, it would take the fire ages to get this far.' He looked down into her face. 'Sure you'll be all right?'

She nodded. 'Just hurry, Ritchie!'

'I'll flag a car down and come back with the driver,' he promised, and began to run, his lithe body loping rapidly across the field towards the main road.

Linzi watched him go, feeling very odd. Her heart was beating much too fast; she felt as if she was weightless, floating. It wasn't the effect of the accident, of the explosion, or the fire now raging across the field they had just left. It was a symptom of something far more disturbing, a trauma that could have serious after-effects.

She had to stop working for Ritchie Calhoun. She saw that suddenly. She had to get away from him. If she didn't, and soon, she would be in danger of falling in love with him, and she was very afraid that Ritchie could be getting interested in her.

Her marriage might be in serious trouble, she might no longer love Barty in quite the way she had once, but he was her husband, and she did still love him. She knew he loved her, too, even when he got drunk and knocked her about. The feeling between them had deep roots, going back many years; he was more than a lover to her, he was the only brother she had ever had, the best friend she had ever had, her only family, as she was his. For all the pain and bitterness of the last two years her marriage was still alive, and she had no intention of walking away from Barty.

She certainly had no intention of getting involved with Ritchie Calhoun. The end result of an affair was always pain, either when it broke up or if it grew more intense, and she had had enough pain in her life already.

A groan made her start and look down at Ted. He was moving, a hand to his head. 'What the hell...?'

'Lie still, Ted,' Linzi said, kneeling beside him again and bending down to smile into his dazed eyes. 'Don't move. Ritchie has gone for help. He won't be long.'

'What happened?' Ted asked, then before she could answer said, 'The chopper! I remember...it crashed, didn't it? Am I imagining it, or did it blow up?'

'It exploded, we all got blown off our feet and you seem to have been hit by flying metal, but Ritchie took a look at you and he says it isn't serious.'

Ted half smiled. 'He took a course in first aid, so he'd know. So that's what's giving me this headache—it's like being a gong; I feel as if someone is beating on my head. I suppose you haven't got an aspirin on you?'

'I'm sorry, Ted,' Linzi said gently, 'I don't think you should take any pills until you see a doctor. Ritchie will get one here as fast as he can.'

Ted grimaced, put his hand to his head again, looked at his fingers and groaned. 'Ugh...blood...I hate the sight of blood, especially my own. It makes me feel weak.'

He tried to lift his head and Linzi said urgently, 'Don't move, Ted, you must keep still.'

'I just wanted to see...is my chopper a write-off?'

She nodded and Ted looked sad.

'Damn. I loved that machine.'

'You'll get another one,' she comforted.

'It won't be the same.' He coughed, frowned, his eyes flickering, then he tried to sit up again. 'Smoke...Linzi, where's that black smoke coming from? Is the chopper still burning?'

'The wheat caught fire...' She stopped as Ted closed his eyes. 'Ted, don't pass out again...talk to me...'

He coughed again, opened his eyes, reached out a hand and gripped her hard when she took it. 'Help me up, Linzi! I'm not lying here waiting to be cooked to a crisp!'

She looked over her shoulder and saw the black smoke pouring up, the flames as crimson as poppies. The fire had changed direction, was spreading their way. Panic streaked through her. Ted staggered to his feet and she slid her arm around his waist, supporting him.

'Lean on me! I'm stronger than I look, I can take your weight.'

They made their way along the wall, working away from the raging fire, keeping close to the reedy, rank ditch which was choked with weeds and the haunt of buzzing insects. They were almost at the far side when Ted reeled and had to sit down again.

Ted was coughing, breathless, shaking. 'I'm only just beginning to realise how close a call that was!' he muttered, putting his head down on his raised knees.

'Don't think about what might have happened; it didn't, we're fine, and you'll be there when the new baby arrives,' Linzi hurriedly said, stroking the tangled, sweat-dampened hair back from his pale face. Blood was trickling down into his eyes, he irritably rubbed it away, and Linzi remembered that she had a packet of make-up wipes in her bag and searched for them. At least she could make Ted a little more comfortable.

The circles of lint were soaked in cool witch-hazel; Ted gave a groan of pleasure as she began delicately cleaning his temples. 'Hmm...that's marvellous... what is it?'

'I take eye make-up off with these little pads,' she explained.

'I suppose you don't have something really useful in that bag of yours, like a bottle of whisky?'

Ted laughed and Linzi smiled a little, too, then, a moment later, heard the engine of some heavy vehicle like a tractor coming through the gate on the far side of the field.

'Is it Ritchie?' asked Ted, and she smiled, her face bright with relief.

'Yes, in a Range Rover—I hope he found a doctor!'

The vehicle moved through the standing wheat; mowing it down. When the Range Rover halted, a large young man wearing cricket whites climbed out, a bag in one hand.

'My patient?' he asked, looking at Ted.

'Yes.' Linzi backed off, leaving him alone with Ted, and Ritchie joined her.

'I was lucky,' he said with a grin. 'I was able to hitch a lift into the village from the local milk lorry. The driver told me I'd find the doctor playing cricket on the village green, he dropped me there and I was just in time to see the doctor bowl someone out. I don't think I was too popular with the rest of the village team, he's their best bowler, but he had his Range Rover there so we were able to get back here fast.'

'I've never been so glad to see anyone!' she admitted, and he smiled down at her, putting an arm around her.

'Are you OK?'

She felt a pulse beating hard in her neck and shifted so that his arm fell. 'Fine,' she said huskily.

'I see you had to move Ted further along—was he conscious then, or did you drag him?'

'He walked, with my help. The fire and smoke seemed to be getting closer.'

Ritchie nodded and walked off to stare across the field they had landed in, his face grim. 'There's a fire engine on the way too,' he said, just as they both heard the clanging of bells. 'Speak of the devil!' Ritchie added.

They watched the fire engine drive into the next field and halt; the firemen leap out in fire gear, looking like robots or aliens from outer space in their breathing apparatus, directing some sort of foam spray at the burning helicopter. They could heard the crackle of walkie-talkies as an officer gave his men orders, then the doctor stood up and came over to them.

'The cut is superficial and he isn't showing any signs of concussion. I'd say he was hit by a flying piece of metal, but it seems to have been a glancing blow. With any luck he'll be fine. We must get him to hospital, though, for X-rays and observation. I can take you all.'

As they drove away Linzi watched the flames dying down, the black smoke rolling over the countryside. 'Fire is a terrifying force,' she thought aloud.

'Very destructive,' agreed the doctor, turning out on to the main road. Gloomily Ted and Ritchie stared back at the burnt-out helicopter.

When they reached the hospital, half an hour's drive away, Ted was whisked away to the X-ray department, and Linzi and Ritchie both had brief check-ups before being told they were fine and could leave. Ted was going to be kept in overnight, at least, and maybe for a few more days.

'The police want to talk to you before you leave, though,' they were told by the young doctor. 'Feel up to it? It would save you the trouble of coming back to be interviewed tomorrow.'

Ritchie looked at Linzi enquiringly. 'I can talk to them alone, if you don't feel you want to face it.'

She shook her head. 'I'm OK.'

'Oh, tough as old boots,' he mocked. 'You look it! Well, first I want to ring Ted's wife and break the news to her myself. I owe her that. The police can wait another five minutes.'

Linzi went into the hospital cloakroom while he was talking to Megan. 'Don't worry, it isn't serious, Megan, you don't need to come tonight. They'll be giving him a sedative to help him sleep. Tomorrow, I'll arrange for a chauffeur-driven car to bring you here and take you home again. Ted may be able to go back with you so bring him some clean clothes.'

Linzi shut the cloakroom door and felt a relief at being alone. She went to the lavatory, and looked at her smoke-blackened face with wry dismay. What a sight!

The water was delicious on her skin; she splashed a lot of cool, clean water on her face, feeling as if it was seeping in through every pore. She was so hot!

Eventually she had to stop washing and dry her face, then she combed her hair, brushed grass and dust off her clothes. Well, she looked a little more normal now.

When she rejoined him Ritchie was talking to a policeman who was writing down what he said. As soon as Linzi appeared, Ritchie broke off and said, 'Can we do this tomorrow? We both feel pretty shattered by the accident and we need to get home.'

'We really need to talk to you tonight,' said the policeman.

'I've told you most of what I can tell you,' protested Ritchie.

The policeman looked at Linzi. 'Can I ask you a few questions, Miss...?'

'Mrs York,' she told him.

He gave her a sharp look, his brows lifting slightly. 'Mrs York,' he repeated, writing the name down. 'I see. And you were in the helicopter with Mr Calhoun?'

'She is my secretary,' Ritchie said curtly, looking suddenly very angry.

'I see, sir,' the policeman said expressionlessly.

Ritchie bit out, 'Ted Hobson, the man who was injured, works for me, too. We were all up here researching for a confidential project. But that has nothing whatever to do with the accident. Until the helicopter has been inspected by a fire team and a flight engineer we won't have any idea what caused the crash. It may be a simple engine failure. But it will take time to determine the cause for certain, and until we know more there is no point in asking us questions.'

'Well, I'm afraid I have to, sir,' said the policeman with polite obstinacy. 'It must have been a very distressing incident, so I won't ask any more questions tonight, but it would help us if you and Mrs York stayed near by tonight and came in to the station to see us tomorrow morning. There's a comfortable country inn not far from here. The Green Man.'

'Yes, we know it. I've been staying there for a few days,' Ritchie said tersely. 'Well, if you insist we hang around in this neighbourhood tonight, very well. We'll be at the Green Man tonight and call in at your station tomorrow morning. But just now Mrs York is as white as a ghost and may pass out altogether if you keep us standing here much longer, so can we go now?'

She was grateful to him for his protective attitude, although she wouldn't have minded answering the police questions. It was typical of Ritchie, though—he was a complex man: tough and hard-working, shrewd and clear-headed, yet capable of being sensitive, thoughtful and kind. No wonder his men thought the world of him. Whenever there was an accident Ritchie took enormous pains to see that an injured man got the best possible treatment, and that his family were equally looked after. His firm had a very good safety record and he was always trying to improve the safety standard of the sites, but on a construction site there were always accidents, as she had soon discovered, some through human error, others through almost wilful carelessness.

He was yawning now. 'My God, I'm tired! What a day this has been! We had better get back to the Green Man; I'll organise a taxi.'

'How far away are we?'

'About four miles off.' Ritchie looked at his watch. 'It's nearly seven. I'd no idea all this had taken so long.' His grey eyes narrowed on her face, probing it. 'Will it be a problem with your husband if you spend the night away from home?'

She flushed, knowing what he was really asking. If only he hadn't seen those bruises, put two and two together and arrived at a far too accurate answer. 'He's away all this week,' she muttered.

His face changed, a crooked smile curving his mouth. 'Well, that makes things easier, doesn't it?'

It did, of course. It was a tremendous relief to know Barty wasn't at home, waiting for her, watching the clock, getting angry and then storming out to get drunk, but she wished Ritchie Calhoun didn't understand that so well.

'The police can't insist that we stay at the Green Man, can they?' she asked hesitantly, and Ritchie gave her a wry glance.

'Not exactly, but, frankly, I shall stay there anyway. I'm half dead on my feet. I don't know about you, but I could do with an early night, and I don't think you should drive all the way back home tonight, only to have to come back tomorrow.'

She couldn't deny she was tired, too, and she saw his point. Looking at him closely, she could see the lines deeply etched into his face; a greyness in his skin, tension in jaw and mouth. They had both had a bad day, but Ritchie had been the one who went to get help; he must be exhausted.

'It isn't wise to drive after a traumatic experience like that one, either,' he added drily, and she sighed, conceding that he was right.

'OK. If I can get a room!'

'I'll ring them, then ring for a taxi,' he said, walking over to a telephone on the wall in the hospital hallway.

It was nearly eight before they reached the Green Man. The taxi was old, the driver older, and very slow. He negotiated the narrow country roads at the pace of an elderly snail. Linzi sat in the corner of the passenger seat, making herself as small as possible in order to stay as far away from Ritchie as she could, and stared out of the window at the green hedges, the trees behind them, in the fields.

The sunset was spectacular, lighting the landscape with a glowing warmth that riveted her attention. The world was beautiful, she had never realised before just how beautiful; all her senses seemed to have been sharpened by coming so close to death. The sky was awash with colour; gold, rose-pink, tender blue, the soft white of clouds.

Her eye followed the rolling green fields to a distant spur of blue-hazed hills, then came back to the hedges they passed, riotous with wild flowers. Dreamily she noted them flash by: pinky-purple foxgloves, as speckled as a snake inside the long bell shape; climbing dog rose, abundant with fragile, very pale pink roses; deep scarlet poppies with blue-black centres, shedding their petals on the road, the lacy, creamy sprays of meadowsweet filling the air with a fragrance like honey, and rose-bay willow-herb which had once brightened the bomb sites of London during the summers of the last war and still grew wherever it could find a space on waste land.

Ritchie made no attempt to talk to her. He sat staring out of his own window, one long leg crossed over the other, his arms folded too. She wondered what he was thinking; whatever it was, it wasn't making him happy. His face was grim.

By the time they got to the Green Man the pub car park was filling up with cars. It was a favourite night spot for townsfolk who liked a drive out to the country on long, hot summer evenings to have dinner, or sit in the beer gardens behind the pub, drinking and talking and listening to music from the bar.

'It quietens down at ten-thirty, when the bars shut,' Ritchie promised as they went up to their own rooms. 'And I've managed to get a table in the restaurant, so how about eating in half an hour? Can you be ready by then? I don't know about you, but I want to have a bath first, I feel as if I've been down a coalmine.'

She gave a faintly hysterical giggle. 'You look it!' His eyes had smudged rims; black smoke dust was etched into the lines on his face.

His expression lightened for a second and he grinned. 'You don't look much better yourself! Don't take too long in your bath, though. I'll tap on your door when I'm ready to go down.'

She didn't have a change of clothes with her, and her white blouse was filthy, so when she had had her bath she only put her red jacket on, buttoning it up to the neck. She washed her blouse out then, and hung it over the bath to drip dry during the night. Just as she finished doing that Ritchie tapped on the door and she joined him.

He ran a comprehensive glance over her, his black brows arching. 'Well, you look a lot better now, but aren't you hot in that jacket?'

'My white shirt was much too dirty to put on again, and I haven't got anything else to wear.'

He grimaced. 'Of course! Stupid me! If you'd mentioned it I could have helped—I could have lent you a clean shirt.' His grey eyes teased. 'Of course, it would have been much too big on you, but it would be cooler than that jacket! Shall I go and get one now?'

She shook her head. 'I'm fine—but if I could borrow one later I'd be grateful. That is... if you don't mind if I...' She broke off, slightly flushed, and his eyes narrowed.

His quick mind worked it out. 'To sleep in?' A derisive little glint showed in the grey eyes. 'You don't like sleeping in the nude?' As her colour deepened he softly said, 'I'll get you a shirt on our way to bed.'

She didn't like the way he said that and stiffened, but then he added calmly, 'Well, let's go and eat.'

The restaurant was only half full, the service swift. Within an hour they were drinking their coffee because neither of them wanted a dessert.

Ritchie looked drawn and pale, but his mind was still working, deciding what to do the next day. 'First thing in the morning, we'll report to this police station, give a formal statement, and then I'll drive you back to the office. I'll have your car picked up by one of my men later in the day.'

She was used to him taking decisions for her, but she quietly suggested, 'Wouldn't it be easier if I drove myself to the police station, and then on to the office?'

'No,' Ritchie firmly told her. 'You may still be in shock tomorrow—there's often a delayed effect from these things. You'd better not risk driving.'

'What about you?' she argued, her eyes wry. 'Why shouldn't you have delayed shock too?'

'I'm used to moments of crisis, they happen all the time in my business. I've been blown up before, when some clown made a mistake setting fuses on a demolition job. I was deaf for days after that. But I'm tough.' His grey eyes brooded on her, then he said huskily, 'Whereas, you're so fragile you look like thistledown; I don't want you getting blown away!'

She lowered her eyes, flushing, oddly breathless.

Ritchie looked at his watch. 'Well, we'd better get some sleep—ready?'

She nodded and got up. When they got upstairs Ritchie told her to wait while he went into his room in search of the clean shirt he had promised her. He reappeared with a clean, neatly pressed shirt in his hand, a new toothbrush still in its case, a tube of toothpaste.

'Anything else you need?'

'No, thank you, I shall be fine.'

'Well, then, goodnight, Linzi,' he said softly. 'Sleep well.'

Her voice husky, she said, 'You too, goodnight.'

He leaned down and before she could move away he lightly brushed a kiss across her mouth. It was nothing like the passionate kiss he had given her after the helicopter crash, in fact it was gentle and soothing rather than sexy, but Linzi found it almost as disturbing.

She might find it moving and comforting, but she had no right to Ritchie's tenderness. She belonged to another man.

But she was too tired to think about that tonight. She was undressed and in bed, wearing Ritchie's crisply laundered shirt, within another five minutes. Within ten she was asleep, but during the night she had troubled dreams.

She kept reliving the crash; no doubt her mind was busily absorbing the fear and shock, dealing with all that trauma: the whirling of the helicopter tumbling out of the sky, the terror of being flung about, landing with that terrifying thud and then Ritchie dragging her and pulling her out of the chopper, forcing her to run, until the explosion blew them both off their feet.

The dreams were so vivid, changed so much, swinging wildly between fear and indifference, relief and the happiness of surviving, the sheer panic with which she watched the scarlet and black of the fire spreading through the wheatfield, and, most intense of all, the moments in Ritchie's arms when their mouths met and she felt the upsurge of an emotion so powerful that it could dominate all her memories of the rest of that traumatic day.

She was still deeply asleep when someone began knocking loudly on her door, followed by Ritchie's voice urgently calling her name.

'Linzi! Linzi! Are you OK?'

She sat up, drowsy-eyed, flushed and dishevelled, looked at her watch and groaned, then scrambled out of bed and padded over, barefoot, to open the door, keeping it on the chain.

Ritchie's frowning face filled the gap, his grey eyes intent on her.

'I'm sorry, I overslept,' she stammered. 'What time is it?'

'Ten past eight. Did you sleep well?'

She nodded. 'Did you?'

'Like a log. How soon can you be ready?'

She noticed suddenly that he was wearing a crisp, blue-striped shirt, a dove-grey silk tie, an elegantly tailored cool grey suit, and looked very different from the way he had looked yesterday when he was wearing jeans and a grass-stained, crumpled shirt. A spark of amusement lit her blue eyes. Ritchie had dressed to convince the police he was a respectable citizen.

'What are you grinning at?' he asked, eyes narrowing.

She smoothed out her expression and demurely said, 'Nothing. I won't take long to dress, give me five minutes!'

'Only five?' He was disbelieving. He ran a glance slowly down over her then, taking in the way she looked in the crisp white shirt he had lent her. It was far too big for her, the shoulders too wide, the sleeves too long. Standing in that doorway she had the early morning sunlight behind her; it illuminated her slender body within the white material, revealed every curve, the high, rounded breasts, the small waist, the smooth slim hips.

Her bare, tanned legs showed beneath the hem of the shirt, her well-shaped calves and small, naked feet.

Linzi blushed under his eyes. 'You can time me. Five minutes!' she said huskily, wished he wouldn't stare.

'Have you any idea how sexy you look in my shirt?' he whispered, and she tensed.

'Don't flirt with me!'

He grimaced. 'Sorry. OK, I'll time you. I'll be downstairs, reading the morning papers. Do you want tea or coffee with your breakfast?'

'Coffee, please.'

'Orange juice?' She nodded and he asked, 'Brown or white toast?'

'Brown, please.'

Ritchie showed her his wristwatch. 'Five minutes, then!'

'Right!' She shut the door and raced into the bathroom. As she ran water to wash her face, she eyed her reflection in the mirror above the sink. Her blue eyes had a dangerous brilliance, and her skin was deeply flushed. Her face betrayed her, and she bleakly recognised that she was going to have to break away from Ritchie Calhoun before it was too late and disaster hit them both. Every day she was getting in deeper; already she was going to find it bitterly hard to say goodbye to him.

Those dreams were a danger signal, for a start. Over and over again during the night she had dreamt of Ritchie kissing her. She turned away to find her brush, running it through her tangled blonde hair, frowning. Well, how did you censor your dreams, for heaven's sake? She couldn't help what her unconscious came up with, could she?

You can stop it having any memories to work on, she grimly told herself as she hurried to get dressed in the clothes she had been wearing yesterday.

She just made it downstairs in five minutes. Ritchie was sitting on his own at a table by a window, his newspaper open and his eyes riveted on a page. He didn't even look up as Linzi sat down.

'I made it, didn't I?' she asked breathlessly.

Ritchie lifted his head. His grey eyes were hard, his face set like stone.

'What's wrong?' Linzi whispered, instantly afraid of bad news. 'Not Ted?'

He shook his head. 'No, Ted's fine, I rang the hospital earlier, and he's probably coming home today. No, it's this . . .'

He threw the newspaper across at her and watched her face as she glanced down at the open page, frowning.

It wasn't a national paper, but it was a provincial newspaper with a big circulation in this part of England. A headline leapt out at her. 'RITCHIE CALHOUN IN CHOPPER CRASH.'

Ritchie was well known throughout the area, so it didn't surprise her that the newspaper should give so much space to his helicopter crashing.

'They got the news in fast!' she commented before she began to read, and then her face drained of colour. She read the piece again before looking up at Ritchie.

'They make it sound . . .'

He nodded. 'As if we'd been staying here together since the weekend! I know.'

Linzi was appalled. 'Why on earth have they done this?'

'Well, I have been staying here, of course,' said Ritchie offhandedly. 'Although I don't know how they found out about that! I can only think a reporter talked to someone at the police station, got the details of the crash from the police, including your name and the fact that you were my secretary, was told we'd be staying here last night, then rang up the Green Man, and was told I'd been a guest there for three days, already. They simply jumped to the conclusion that you had, too.'

That made sense, and yet... 'It's the way they've written it...' Linzi said unhappily.

Ritchie was a well-known figure right across the middle of England; he was wealthy and influential and had had a number of girlfriends, none of whom had so far managed to get him to the altar. The Press found Ritchie fascinating; they often gossiped about his love life. Obviously, they'd taken it for granted that Linzi was having an affair with him, and, without risking a libel case, the newspaper had sailed pretty close to hinting that she and Ritchie were lovers.

'What on earth are we going to do?' she thought aloud, reading the story again and even more horrified.

Ritchie gave her a frowning, searching look. 'If your husband sees that might it cause trouble?'

White to the lips, Linzi nodded.

'But he's away, isn't he?' Ritchie slowly said.

'In Manchester,' she told him.

'Well, I don't think this paper circulates there, so he isn't likely to see the story.'

Ritchie was infuriatingly casual about it, dismissing her anxiety as meaningless, but Linzi remained worried all day. She kept praying that Barty would not see the story. She was afraid of his reaction. She had been hungry when she woke up, but now she wasn't hungry any more.

She didn't eat any breakfast, just drank some strong black coffee before they went to the police station. A reporter was hanging about when they emerged, but Ritchie brushed him off without too much trouble.

Two hours later they arrived back at their office and Linzi had to face the fascinated curiosity of all the other girls, who had heard about the crash, it seemed, on local radio news early that morning.

Linzi winced. What chance was there that Barty wouldn't hear about it?

'I'd have been petrified!' Petal said, staring at her as if she had grown two heads. 'When it was going down, you must have thought you were going to be killed!'

'I did,' Linzi admitted. But she hadn't been scared, she remembered; a strange sort of fatalism had gripped her. She had almost, crazy though it seemed, been glad; relieved, anyway. As if fate was taking care of all her problems at one stroke.

And yet, afterwards, there had been a moment of intense happiness, a new sense of the beauty of the world, the possibilities of life...

'It was a miracle you didn't get killed,' Petal told her, as if she might not have realised that, and Linzi laughed rather wildly.

Ritchie was out of the office again that afternoon, but returned at five and asked Linzi to work for a further hour or so. 'I'm sorry, I know you must be tired, but I won't keep you long this time,' he promised, looking with compunction at her pale face.

She wryly shrugged. 'I'll manage. Don't worry about me, I'm tougher than I look.'

His eyes were brilliant and tender. 'Impossible! No woman could be that tough!'

The gentle mockery made her laugh, a little unsteadily.

'And you haven't got your car yet, have you?' Ritchie added, smiling. 'I'm sorry, I forgot all about it, but I've made arrangements now for it to be driven back to-morrow morning, and tonight I'll drive you home myself.'

'There's no need, I can get a bus . . .'

'Don't be silly, it's no problem to me,' he insisted. 'Now, can you find me the Lambett contracts?'

It was seven before they left the office and Ritchie quietly asked, 'As it's so late, will you have dinner with me?'

She had been half expecting it. He knew her husband was away. She didn't look at him, her pale face averted, just shook her head. 'I can't, I must go home. If my husband rings I want to be there.'

All day she had been on tenterhooks, her nerves stretched to breaking point, in case Barty might walk in, in one of his savage tempers because he had heard about the chopper crashing, and about her staying at the Green Man with Ritchie overnight. She was in no mood to go out to dinner and pretend to be calm, not while she knew Barty might arrive home at any minute.

'We have to talk,' Ritchie said roughly.

She stiffened, still not looking at him. 'What about?' But she knew, before he answered, and her stomach plummeted.

'You and me,' he said in a deep, harsh voice.

'No, Ritchie,' she whispered. 'Don't... don't say any more. You mustn't. I can't listen, I don't want you to say anything.'

'OK, we won't talk about us, but whatever happens you can't stay with him, Linzi,' Ritchie muttered, giving her a look that she felt even though she had turned away from him. 'The man's going to hurt you badly one day, if he goes on hitting you, you know that. Why stay with him and wait for it to happen?'

'He's my husband and I love him. I'm not discussing him with you, Ritchie.' She swallowed and on a wave of sheer misery said, 'I can't go on working for you, this can't go on, I should have left long ago. You know I should. I'll give formal notice on Monday.'

Ritchie pulled up outside her home and sat staring ahead, his long fingers drumming on the wheel. She reached for the door-handle to get out and he suddenly broke out, 'Don't go, Linzi! I've got to tell you how I feel, I'm going crazy...'

Her heart hurt and she could barely breathe, torn between a strange joy and that aching grief. 'Don't!' she muttered. 'Can't you see, that's why I must go?'

She heard his long-drawn breath. 'You know how I feel,' he said very quietly. 'Don't you, Linzi?' A little silence and the harsh drag of his breathing grew faster, then he whispered, 'Linzi, do you——?'

'No,' she said wildly. 'Ritchie, don't! I can't bear any more,' and, on the point of tears, she dived out of the car.

She didn't stop running until she got to her front door. As she put her key into the lock the door opened from the other side, and her heart stopped as she saw Barty looming there.

'Barty!' She froze in the doorway, biting her inner lip.

He was in shirt-sleeves, his tie off and his collar undone, his hair dishevelled, his face darkly flushed. From the way he stood there, on his heels, swaying slightly, she knew at once that he had been drinking.

'You're back early,' she said uneasily, trying to smile but beginning to be frightened of the darkness in his staring eyes.

'Not expecting me, eh?' he muttered thickly, his speech slurred. 'W...while the c...cat's away the mice will play! Don't think I don't know what *you've* been playing at! I've read all about it, I know everything, so don't bother to lie to me this time!'

He raised his arm and she saw the newspaper clenched in his hand; he threw it at her, snarling. 'In black and white, you treacherous little...it's all there, in black and white!'

She was so scared that her wits deserted her, she could only stammer helplessly. 'B...Barty, I...it w...wasn't like that, not the way the newspaper made it sound...Ritchie and I weren't staying there together——'

'Liar!' His hand flew out before she knew it was coming; the blow sent her stumbling back into the wall, then before she could pull herself together he hit her again, even harder, and her ears rang, her head starting to go round dizzily.

Barty bent towards her, said through his teeth, 'This is the end of all the lying, Linzi. You're going to admit it, this time! He's your lover...isn't he?' But he hit her again as she tried to answer, to deny it. 'Isn't he?' his remorseless voice demanded. 'He's your lover, isn't he, you little——?'

'*No*!' she screamed, and then, before he could hit her again, she tried to get away, to run, down the corridor to the bathroom, to lock herself in there, as she had sometimes in the past. If she could get there he might go on drinking until he passed out!

When he woke up he would be morose but sober, suffering with a hangover, but in that state usually more amenable to reason. When he was drunk his inhibitions broke down, and up from the depths of his pysche rose dark monsters of grief and frustration, but Linzi never forgot that even the monsters were an expression of Barty's love for her.

Sober, Barty would never hurt her. If she could only get to the bathroom...

This time, though, her reflexes were slower because she was shaking so hard that she couldn't run fast. Barty caught her before she could get far.

'Where do you think you're going? Back to him? Oh, no, you don't! You won't be seeing him again! Do you hear me? I'll never let you go to him again!'

Then he began beating her with a black ferocity before which she was utterly helpless. She had discovered, long ago, that at a certain point his violence seemed to freeze her, paralyse her, so that she couldn't even try to stop him, let alone either fight him or plead with him. White-faced and trembling, she didn't even cry as he forced her back, across their little sitting-room, his blows falling relentlessly.

She just put her arms over her face, to protect her head, like a cowering child, crouching in a corner of the room.

Barty knocked her arms down, then his hands closed round her throat; he held her off the ground, her toes kicking air as she struggled.

Bending towards her, his face an inch from hers, he hissed, 'I've had enough, Linzi, I can't take any more of this... if I can't have you, he can't... I'll kill you first...'

He meant it. She saw it in his staring, dilated eyes. Barty was going to kill her.

She had often thought it might end this way. At times she had even hoped for it, might have welcomed it as one way out of what seemed a hopeless situation.

His hands squeezed her throat; she couldn't breathe. Gasping for air as his grip tightened, she was in agony. Instinctively she reached up to unclasp his hands, but Barty had always been stronger. She heard her breath rasping in her throat, or was she sobbing, trying to talk to him? Her blue eyes pleaded.

'Barty, please . . . darling, don't . . .' she tried to beg, but all that emerged were those strange, hoarse, choking sounds.

She was going to die. The thought seemed incredible, unreal—and then panic surged up inside her. A voice clamoured inside her head. She didn't want to die . . . she wanted to live . . .

Her tongue seemed to be filling her mouth; her mind was clouding. She felt consciousness slowly slipping away, her body going limp. With a pang of shock she realised that she was dying . . . this was it, this weakness, the confusion of her mind and senses . . . this was death . . .

CHAPTER FOUR

SOMEWHERE in the darkness that followed Linzi heard a voice. 'Oh, no... oh, my God, no!' She was incurious about it. It didn't seem to have anything to do with her. She was drifting far away in a cold place; she didn't have either the desire or the energy to get back.

Someone somewhere was breathing, rapidly, roughly, as if they had been running; she tried to ignore them because if she didn't they would drag her back and she didn't want to go back. She had escaped; she didn't quite know from what, only that she did not want to go back. It was safer here. It was quiet. Nobody hassled or tried to hurt her.

'Don't die, Linzi... I couldn't bear it!' the voice said, much closer to her, sounding anguished.

She didn't want emotion breaking in on her peace. She frowned irritably, her thin brows flickering.

'Ah...' There was a quick, indrawn breath, then someone picked up her wrist and held it carefully, finger and thumb pressed into her blue vein. He was looking for a pulse, she dimly understood. Was there one? Hadn't her heart stopped beating yet? She was sure it had. It must have done—she was dead, wasn't she? How long did it take to die?

There was a long sigh, then a hand touched her face, gently, brushing the curve of her cold cheek, and she

79

thought: Can you feel a touch if you're dead? Can you hear the living?

'You're alive...' the deep, husky voice murmured. 'Oh, Linzi...I thought for one terrible minute you were dead, but you're alive...'

No. He was wrong. She was dead. She remembered dying.

'Wake up, Linzi,' he whispered, warm lips moving on her pale, closed lids.

Her whole body flinched away from that light touch. She knew who had kissed her and she gave a weak, protesting sigh. Why couldn't he leave her alone? She didn't want to wake up. She was frightened of opening her eyes. She preferred being dead. If she woke up she would have to face...something...something she didn't quite remember but which she sensed was still there, waiting to leap out at her.

She couldn't quite remember what had happened before she fell into this darkness, only that there had been pain and grief and terror, and that if she let herself come back to life it would all be there, waiting for her, again.

'Linzi, for God's sake!' The deep voice was urgent, sounded almost desperate. Hands took hold of her shoulders and lifted her off the floor; an arm slid underneath her, the warmth of it striking through what she was wearing. 'Say something...wake up!'

The change of position made her cough, and coughing hurt her raw, swollen throat.

'It hurts...my throat...' she moaned, her long, darkened lashes stirring against her white cheeks.

'Don't talk, then; but open your eyes!' he urged.

His will was so strong that she slowly, reluctantly obeyed, to find him kneeling beside her, supporting her with one arm, bending over her, his face close to hers. Fear and panic cramped her insides and she pushed him away weakly.

'No! What are you doing, Ritchie? Are you mad? Barty will kill you if he finds you here! You shouldn't have come! Please...go away...'

She tried to get up but her legs were weak underneath her; she stumbled and almost fell over again. As she clutched at a nearby chair to support herself, she caught sight of Barty, lying on the floor a few feet away.

Linzi froze in shock. What was he doing on the floor? Had he had a fight with Ritchie? Had Ritchie knocked him out?

And then she noticed the dark blood matting his brown hair, blood crawling slowly down his white, cold face.

'Barty!' she shuddered, clutching at the chair-back. 'Barty... My God...what...what...?'

She threw herself down beside him, shivering, trembling. He wasn't moving. He didn't open his eyes to look at her as she called his name. There was blood trickling down into his lashes; she sobbed drily as she bent down to kiss his lips.

'Darling...oh, Barty, wake up...'

His mouth was cold and stiff. She lifted her head to look at him again, her blue eyes glazed and enormous; her blood ran cold at the strange immobility of his body. His chest wasn't rising and falling. She tried to listen for the sound of his breathing but panic made her heart beat too fast, deafening her.

'Barty! Barty!' she cried out, and tried to lift him up, but his body was too heavy for her; he was a dead weight in her hands.

She looked down at him, eyes wild and wide, shaking him.

'Stop it, Linzi!' Ritchie said curtly. 'There's no use. He's dead.'

A strangled cry broke from her. 'No! Don't say that, don't tell me that, he isn't, not dead...not dead...Barty...wake up, Barty!'

She caught his wrist, searched for a pulse; found nothing, put her head on his chest, trying to hear a heartbeat, all the time sobbing breathlessly, trembling.

Ritchie tried to pull her away, up to her feet, and she resisted him, shaking her head, her long, silvery hair swinging around her pale, shocked face, her lids like bruised violets.

'Let me alone!'

'You can't do anything for him, Linzi!' Ritchie's face was grim, his voice rough. 'I tell you...he's dead!'

'Don't say that! He isn't. He can't be. We must be able to do something! A doctor...we must get a doctor...we must get an ambulance...take him to a hospital...'

She turned towards the phone, and that was when she saw the old brass candlestick that her Aunt Ella had given her for a wedding present. It was one of a pair which always stood on a small table by the window. Now it lay on the floor, a foot or two from Barty, and there was dark blood smearing the solid pedestal foot of it.

Linzi stared dumbly at it for a second. It felt as if eternity passed. She looked at the candlestick and then at Barty, and then she looked slowly up at Ritchie, who was very pale, his face harsh.

'Don't look like that!' he said in a low voice. 'He was trying to kill you, he'd all but choked the life out of you! He had to be stopped!'

'You killed him...' she whispered, her mouth even whiter than her skin. 'Oh, God, my poor Barty! You killed him——'

From the open door of the flat came a gasp and Ritchie spun round. The woman from the flat next door stood there, staring round-eyed with curiosity. She took in Barty on the floor, covered in blood; Linzi kneeling beside him; then her eyes moved to Ritchie. An odd succession of reactions went across her face: shock, horror, then suddenly fear; she began to scream and stumbled out again, screaming.

Icy coldness engulfed Linzi: she fell forward across Barty in a dead faint.

The next time she opened her eyes the flat seemed to be full of people. She was lying on the couch although she had no idea how she had got there. Nobody was taking any notice of her; she half lifted her head to stare around the room. What had happened? Who were all these people? She recognised her next-door neighbour, talking to a man in a uniform. Linzi's dazed eyes took in the familiar blue serge, the shiny buttons. Policemen, she registered. What were they doing here? Another policeman was talking to Ritchie, who was very pale and looked grim. Linzi felt a shiver run through her. A memory pricked: faint and disturbing, something about...Barty?

Barty? she thought, moving slightly, and then someone in white bent over her.

'How do you feel now, Mrs York?'

Ritchie turned sharply. She felt his grey eyes touch her and trembled, looking away from him.

'Barty?' she whispered, searching the room for him.

There was a shape on the floor, covered with a white sheet. Linzi began to scream, tried to sit up.

'Barty!'

Ritchie took a step towards her; one of the policemen caught hold of his arms and held him back. Linzi had sensed his movement. She looked at him with stricken eyes.

'He's dead, isn't he?' Hysteria welled up inside her and she sobbed tearlessly, her voice ragged. 'He's dead and you killed him!'

Ritchie seemed to grow even paler, his grey eyes so dark that they looked almost black; but he didn't speak, just stared at her.

'After everything he had had to go through, it's so cruel!' she accused, as if blaming Ritchie for everything that had happened to Barty. 'What sort of life did he have? The crash...losing his mother...the baby...' Her voice broke off and she groaned achingly. 'The baby...that hurt him more than anything, I think. Hurt us both. Our baby, dying before it was even born! It's so unfair—why did all those things happen to us? Why us? What had we done to deserve it all? And now he's dead. Oh, God, I wish I'd never seen you...never taken that job...if I'd never set eyes on you, Barty would be alive...' Her voice rose wildly, she stared at the covered shape on the floor, her face distraught. 'It's all my fault, isn't it? He's dead because of me! Oh, I can't bear it...I shall go mad...'

One of the policeman had a notebook in his hand; he was writing rapidly.

'What do you mean, Mrs York, it's all your fault? Why do you say that?'

Ritchie turned on him angrily. 'Can't you see what sort of state she's in? Leave her alone, for God's sake!'

The doctor intervened. 'I agree. She can't answer any questions tonight. I'm going to have to sedate her. She's in no condition to give you sensible answers to your questions, anyway.'

He bent down towards Linzi. She shrank away as she saw the hypodermic needle in his hand.

'This isn't going to hurt!' he soothed, deftly rubbing her bare arm with a little pad, and she made a noise somewhere between a sob and wild laughter.

'Isn't going to hurt? Don't bother to lie. Everything hurts. Unless you're dead...the hurting stops then... I wish I were dead...oh, Barty...'

The words faded into each other, the room was fading too, and her eyes closed gratefully as she escaped back into oblivion.

The police spoke to her the following day, in a small, quiet room in the local hospital. One of the police was a young woman with short, dark hair and a calm face;

the other was a man in his late forties with a thin, clever face and shrewd eyes. Linzi watched them bring chairs close to the bed. She lay, very still, almost as white as the sheets; her eyes dark pools of grief and misery in her bruised and battered face. She knew how she looked: she had seen herself in a mirror that morning but the usual dismay and embarrassment she would have felt, knowing what others must think, no longer bothered her. How she looked didn't matter.

'How are you feeling this morning, Mrs York? I'm Superintendent Rogers, and this is Sergeant Dale. I'm sorry to have to trouble you at this time, but I hope you'll understand the urgency of finding out exactly how your husband died, and why we have to talk to you.'

Linzi nodded bleakly. 'I understand.'

'Good, thank you. Now, suppose you tell us, in your own words, exactly what happened yesterday from the moment when you arrived home.'

Huskily she said, 'Barty was very angry with me, he had misunderstood something he'd read in a newspaper...'

The superintendent opened a folder he held on his knee and showed her a grey photocopy of a page from a newspaper. 'This one, Mrs York?'

Startled, she looked at the headline, winced, nodded. 'Your husband believed what he'd read?'

She bit her lip, nodded again. 'He...Barty...was...'

'Jealous?'

A wisp of colour crept into her cheeks. 'He had no reason to be...it was all lies...but he had been drinking. He was upset...' Her voice trailing away, she stared at the neat coverlet over the bed, her hands closing and unclosing, and the police watched her.

Superintendent Rogers prompted her, 'He hit you?'

She nodded without looking up.

'Did he often hit you, Mrs York?'

'Only when he'd been drinking,' she whispered, then looked up wildly, her blue eyes wide and angry. 'Barty loved me, he didn't mean to hurt me, he was always sorry afterwards, it hurt him when he saw...'

'Saw what he'd done to you?' The police were looking at her face: the cut below her eye, the angry bruises, a red swelling along her cheekbones, puffiness around her swollen lips, the deep-sunk dark bruises on her throat, where the fingers had sunk into her flesh. She bore the visible marks of Barty's rage. Linzi felt their stares and winced.

'You mustn't think... Barty was a kind man, I've known him most of my life, he was my best friend as well as my husband. We were very happy until the accident.' She told them about the crash, how Barty's mother had died of the shock, how she had then miscarried the child she was expecting, and the grey months that had followed while Barty was in hospital.

'After that he was never the same again. He was bitter and unhappy and he started to drink.'

There was a silence then Superintendent Rogers asked, 'How did your husband feel about you working for Mr Calhoun?'

'It was far more money, he was pleased when I got the job.' But her eyes didn't meet the policeman's.

Gently he asked, 'Until he became jealous of Mr Calhoun?'

'He resented the long hours I had to work. Mr Calhoun is often out of the office for most of the day, and when he got back he liked me to be there, to work with him on confidential matters. He didn't like to use a Dictaphone in case it got into the wrong hands; I had to be there in the office to work straight on to the computer, while he dictated; then after I'd printed out the documents I'd erase the tape and he would keep the documents in his safe.'

'How often did you work late in this way?'

'Several nights a week.'

'How late did you work?'

'I don't know, I never kept an eye on the clock.' Her voice was edgy, unsteady. 'But quite late, I suppose. It was part of the job, though. When I took it, Ritchie…Mr Calhoun…made it plain that I'd be working odd hours, I'd have to be flexible—take time off during the day, for instance, if I had to work very late. I got paid very well for accepting those conditions.'

Drily the Superintendent said, 'But your husband didn't like it?'

She gave a little sigh, nodding.

The policeman's eyes probed her face; she felt he saw far too much. 'He resented it, in fact, and became jealous of Mr Calhoun? He suspected it wasn't exclusively work that was keeping you out so late?'

A dark flush crawled up her face; she met the man's eyes with anxious defiance. 'Sometimes he said wild things, when he was drunk, but he knew it wasn't true, it was only because he couldn't...since his accident he hadn't been able to...make love...' She drew a long, painful breath. 'It had a terrible effect on him, he felt...he was very bitter.'

The policeman's steady gaze shifted slightly, as if touched by her distress. There was a little silence, giving her time to pull herself together again.

'Are you saying your husband was impotent?' he gently asked.

She nodded, eyes down, wishing she hadn't blurted it out like that. He didn't have to know that. That had nothing to do with what happened. Did it?

'What effect did his inability to make love have on you, Mrs York?' the policeman asked, and she looked up again, her face blank for a moment.

'On me?' Then she realised what he meant and her flush deepened. 'Oh. Oh...well, yes, I was...it wasn't easy for me, either. Obviously.'

'You're young, and very attractive...it would be only natural for you to be frustrated and unhappy. And Mr Calhoun is a very attractive man, a virile man, I'd imagine, a strong, active man with a strong sex drive. And he was in love with you.'

She turned to stone. Stared at the policeman with eyes that didn't see him.

Then, 'No!' she whispered, shaking her head. 'No, no, no. He isn't. You've no right to say that. It's a lie. There was never anything between me and...and Mr Calhoun. I loved my husband and I've been totally faithful to him.'

The calm policeman's eyes watched her dispassionately, without surprise or any hint of sitting in judgement; sieving the evidence, weighing up the possibilities of truth or lies.

'But Mr Calhoun is in love with you, Mrs York.'

Her eyes betrayed her shock. The sharp intake of her breath, the tension of her body. She went on shaking her head, her lips parted but no sound coming out.

'He says he is,' Superintendent Rogers said.

'No!' she hoarsely denied, putting her hands over her ears as if to shut out the quiet, remorseless voice. 'No, no, no!' Her voice rose shrilly, high-pitched.

The policewoman was frowning, looking uneasy, shifting on her chair. The superintendent glanced sideways at her and met her eyes. He grimaced at her. The policewoman got up and poured a glass of water, held it out to Linzi, who shakily took it, almost spilling the contents as she tilted the glass to her mouth.

The water was cool, her lips were dry and hot. She drank, her eyes half closed.

There was a brief pause, she put the glass down on her bedside table and the superintendent resumed the questioning.

'Let us go back to yesterday evening, when you returned home from the office and found your husband waiting for you. Go on from where he began attacking you...'

'I can't, I don't know what happened after that. Barty had his hands around my throat...'

'He tried to strangle you?'

'He didn't know what he was doing! He wouldn't have...he didn't mean, he just lost control, it was the drink. Anyway, I must have fainted. When I came to Barty was...w...was on the floor...' She swallowed. 'He was...was...dead...but I don't know how, what had happened.'

'But Mr Calhoun was there?'

She nodded.

'Had he been there before you lost consciousness?'

She shook her head, a puzzled look in her strained blue eyes. 'No, the last I saw of him he was driving home. I don't know how he came to be in the flat.'

Superintendent Rogers asked, 'Can you remember...was the front door of your flat open or shut?'

She struggled to remember. The details of the evening were blurred in her mind. 'When I got home, I was just going to unlock the front door, I had my key in my hand...when B...Barty...' Tears filled her eyes. 'Sorry...' She searched for a paper tissue, wiped her eyes and blew her nose, then cleared her throat and went on huskily, 'My husband opened the front door before I unlocked it, and I don't remember him closing it.'

'So that it is possible that Mr Calhoun could have walked into the flat and been a witness to your husband's violent treatment of you?'

'I suppose that's what must have happened.'

'When were you first aware of his presence in the flat?'

'Not until I came to, I was lying on the floor, and R...Mr Calhoun was kneeling beside me—that was the first I knew of him being there.'

The quiet voice was deceptively casual. 'And when you came to, were you aware that your husband was dead?'

'No, I thought Barty must have gone out or something, I told Ritchie to go quickly, before Barty came back and found him, I was afraid Barty might kill him if he saw him with me, and then I suddenly saw Barty, on the floor... I didn't realise he was dead even then, I didn't understand... then I saw the blood on his face. I tried to get him to wake up, but he was so cold and heavy, I couldn't move him. Ritchie told me to leave him, he said, "he's dead" but I wouldn't believe it. I tried to make Barty wake up, and then I saw the candlestick.' She broke off, shuddering.

'And you realised how your husband had been killed?' She nodded.

'Did you accuse Mr Calhoun of killing your husband?' She nodded, didn't speak, mouth a white line.

'Why did you do that, Mrs York?'

'He told me he had! He said Barty had been trying to kill me, and he had had to stop him.' She looked at them miserably. 'He didn't mean to kill Barty... I think it was an accident, he just picked up the nearest object and hit out.'

It was the truth. She had had to tell them, for Barty's sake—she owed him the truth. And yet she felt guilty, a sense of betrayal and desolation weighing her down. Barty was dead and Ritchie Calhoun's life might well be ruined, all because of her. Both men would have been better off if they had never met her, yet she had never knowingly hurt either of them. Merely by existing she had caused them pain, and Linzi ached with regret and misery.

'Yes, the brass candlestick,' the policeman said. 'Did you handle it that evening, Mrs York? We have found blurred sets of fingerprints all over it. Some were your husband's, there was a clear set of Mr Calhoun's fingerprints, and a third set... would that be yours?'

She gave them a puzzled look. 'I don't know, I can't remember handling it that night, but I was the one who did the polishing, so my fingerprints would be on it, I suppose.'

'We would like to take your fingerprints to help us eliminate them from our enquiries, Mrs York. Would you mind if we did that now?'

She shook her head, indifferent.

It only took a few moments, and after she had washed her hands she whispered, 'What's going to happen?'

'Mr Calhoun will be charged with murder,' Superintendent Rogers told her, and she gasped, white to her hairline.

'It wasn't murder! I tell you he didn't mean to kill Barty—he thought Barty was trying to strangle me, he was only trying to save my life!'

'So you said, and it may well be that the Director of Public Prosecutions will decide to change the charge to one of manslaughter, but that isn't my decision.'

She bit her lip, staring ahead into a bleak future— there would be a court case, Ritchie would be tried for killing her husband and she would have to give evidence in public, talk about all the things she had desperately tried to hide for so long. She would be accused, condemned, even if she wasn't on trial herself... whatever she said, however loud her protests of innocence, the world would find her guilty of betraying her husband and finally causing his death, and Linzi half accepted that verdict already.

Nobody could blame her as harshly as she blamed herself; she was so ridden by guilt that she didn't really care what happened to her now.

Oh, Barty! she thought, tears burning behind her lids. My poor Barty, you didn't deserve this...

CHAPTER FIVE

THEY kept Linzi in hospital for several weeks; she was allowed no visitors at first and was kept heavily sedated, drifting in and out of chaotic dreams, nightmares in which it happened again, over and over, as if she still couldn't believe it was true, was trying to make herself believe it. Things didn't always happen in the right order, they came in muddled flashes: the helicopter crash, Ritchie's kiss, her own wild response to it, all mixed up in sequence with Barty's outburst, his violence, the moments when she knew he was going to kill her this time and then the blackness that had descended and the awakening to find him dead and Ritchie there with that look of shock on his white, drawn face.

Each time she woke up at that point, sat up in bed staring at nothing, breathing jaggedly, sobbing.

Sometimes she hated Ritchie. She wished she had never met him. She could never forgive him for Barty's death. He might not have meant to kill Barty, he might have walked in and found Barty apparently choking her to death and acted without thinking—logic might tell her that it was unfair to blame Ritchie . . . but she did. If it weren't for him Barty would be alive. That was all she could think about. He had grabbed up that candlestick and hit Barty so hard that Barty had died of it.

Sometimes she would give such an anguished cry that a nurse would run into the room, talk soothingly, give Linzi another injection which would send her back to sleep only to have the cycle repeat itself—the dreams, the waking, the crying.

During the second week she spent more time awake; sitting up by the window of her room staring out in frozen white-faced silence. She couldn't eat, despite the coaxing of the staff. She couldn't concentrate on any of the magazines or books they brought her. If they put on the television she sat and stared blankly at it without noticing what programme was on at the time.

One day a nurse walked into her room and said, 'You have a visitor, Linzi, isn't that nice? Your aunt has come to see you.'

Linzi stared blankly. 'My aunt? I don't have an aunt.'

The nurse looked unsure. 'She says she is your aunt Ella.'

'Aunt Ella!' Linzi's face changed, a faint glimmer of life in her blue eyes. 'I'd forgotten her . . . she isn't really my aunt, she's my father's cousin, and my godmother, I haven't seen her for years, not since my mother's funeral. How did she know I was in hospital?'

The nurse gave her an odd glance. 'Does it matter? She's come to see you, so shall I send her in?'

Linzi had the vaguest memory of Aunt Ella, she wouldn't have bet on being able to recognise her in the street, but the minute she walked into the room Linzi knew her with a start of surprise.

She was tall for a woman, around five feet eight, well built, wearing a tweed skirt and jacket and a blue blouse, and looked competent and sensible, her fair hair mostly grey now but having once been very like Linzi's; a colouring which came from Linzi's father's family. Her blue eyes had faded, too, and were set in a web of laughter-lines.

'Aunt Ella!' Linzi said, her mouth quivering into a smile as the older woman came over to the bed and bent to kiss her cheek. 'You haven't changed a bit!'

'Kind of you, and I wish it were true, but I'm a good few years older than when we last met,' Aunt Ella gruffly said, sitting down on a chair beside the bed. 'How are you? You look like a ghost. Are they looking after you properly?'

Linzi nodded indifferently. She wouldn't have noticed if the staff hadn't treated her well, but in fact they all went out of their way to try to cheer her up.

Aunt Ella leaned over and patted her hand heavily. 'I came as soon as I read the papers, but they wouldn't let me see you then.'

'Newspapers? It's been in the newspapers?' Shock darkened Linzi's blue eyes. It hadn't occurred to her that the Press would pick up on the story. What had the newspapers been saying? she wondered, biting her lip.

'You've had a bad time, haven't you?' Aunt Ella said in a surprisingly gentle voice for such a big woman.

Linzi stared down at the coverlet on the bed, nervously picking at a loose thread in the weave.

Aunt Ella patted her hand again. 'No, set your mind at rest, I'm not here out of curiosity, I shan't ask you any questions about what happened. My only concern is you, my dear. I blame myself for losing touch after your father's death. I am your godmother, after all. I promised your father I'd always take care of you and I didn't, just because I didn't get on with your mother.'

Linzi remembered then how much her mother had disliked Aunt Ella. Whenever she visited them her mother had dropped biting comments on her, not always out of earshot.

'I was very fond of your father,' Aunt Ella said frankly. 'And your mother was a little bit jealous because we were so close. If we hadn't been first cousins, you know, we might have got married, before he met your mother. But in those days first cousins never married, it was frowned upon, so we both married other people and were both very happy, but your mother never quite trusted me.' She grinned a little mischievously and Linzi faintly smile, too.

'Mum was very possessive,' she recalled, and Aunt Ella nodded.

'I know. It was a very happy marriage, just as mine was! My own husband died not long before your father, and maybe that should have brought your mother and me closer together, but it didn't. She was grieving and she resented me because I grieved too. Well, never mind, that's all in the past. I only wish I hadn't let that keep me from getting to know you—but I want to make that up to you. You must be feeling very lonely, but I'm here now, Linzi. You won't have to go through this alone.'

'You're very kind,' whispered Linzi.

Aunt Ella stayed half an hour, talking to her. 'When they let you out of here, do you want to go back to your old home?'

Linzi shivered and shook her head involuntarily. She couldn't bear the idea of going back to the flat she had shared w... Barty.

'Of cou... ...unt Ella quickly said. 'Too many memories. And you w... ...vant to go on with that job, either, will you?'

Linzi's face darkened with stricken colour at the very idea of going back to Ritchie Calhoun's office. Aunt Ella didn't wait for her to reply. No doubt her expression had answered for her.

'Then come to us. I've spoken to the police and they would have no objection to you leaving the area, so long as they had your new address and a guarantee that you will turn up in court. As I just told you, I've got an antique shop in a village not far from Stratford-upon-Avon. Tiny village called Rushmere. A couple of hundred people and a few dogs! But we get good passing trade—people on their way to Stratford often stop, and we do rather well, financially. If you want it, there's a job for you there, for as long as you like. It won't pay as well as Mr Calhoun did, no doubt, but I can throw in free accommodation. I've got a spare bedroom in my house and you're welcome to that, or if you prefer to be independent you might like to live in the flat over the shop, but to begin with why not try staying with me in my house, so that Gareth and I can get to know you?'

'Gareth?'

'My son,' Aunt Ella said on a note of reproach. 'Don't you remember him? He was only a few years older than you—surely you remember Gareth? You used to go swimming with him.'

Linzi remembered him then and smiled faintly. 'Of course, he's fair, with blue eyes! People often used to think he was my big brother—we looked alike.'

Aunt Ella nodded. 'That's right. You both have the Erickson colouring; your father always swore ours was a Viking family from way back and that was why we were all tall, fair and blue-eyed. Gareth married a blonde girl, too, but she died a couple of years ago. She had a weak heart. They had a little boy, Paul, who was only four when she died. Gareth couldn't cope with him on his own so he and Paul came to me so that I could look after them both. I expect Gareth will get married again some day, but meanwhile, I have a big house, there's plenty of room, and Paul is at school all day now. You'll like him, he's a cheerful little boy, and you and Gareth always got on well. As for the village, well, it's a friendly little place; the people are kind. I'm sure you'll soon feel at home there.'

Linzi felt faintly dazed. This morning when she got up she hadn't had an idea what she was going to do when she left hospital, she hadn't even thought ahead that far, and now her life was mapped out for her.

'You're very kind,' she murmured again, her voice husky, and Aunt Ella gave her a searching look.

'If you don't want to come and stay, say so, dear. I won't be offended. I'm just offering a bolthole, if you want it! You aren't obliged to accept.'

Being given the freedom to choose made Linzi's mind up; she gave Aunt Ella a shaky little smile. 'I'm very grateful, and I'd love to come.'

A few days later Linzi was allowed to leave the hospital. Aunt Ella offered to go to the flat and pack up her things, but Linzi nerved herself to do it. She couldn't go on hiding from everything forever. The physical signs of what happened had gone—the bruises and dark stains on her skin had faded, her throat no longer hurt, her voice wasn't hoarse any more, and she could swallow without pain.

The mental scars would never heal. She would have to learn to live with them.

She stopped off *en route* at the local department store to buy two new suitcases and as she was putting them into her car a voice said uncertainly behind her, 'Linzi?'

Swinging, she looked into Megan Hobson's face with a disconcerted intake of breath. 'Oh. Hello.' A spot of red burnt in her cheeks, and she looked away. Megan would know all about it; the whole firm would know the details by now. Painful embarrassment made it hard to look at the other woman, let alone talk to her.

'So you're out of hospital! I tried to see you several times but they said you couldn't have visitors. Did you get my flowers?'

Linzi didn't know; she had been sent flowers from all sorts of surprising people, for a while her little room had looked like a florist's shop, but she hadn't even read the cards. Most of the time she had barely noticed the flowers themselves. She had not been noticing anything very much.

'Yes, thank you,' she lied, though, because she did not want to hurt Megan's feelings. 'It was very kind of you.'

'Not at all, I was very shocked when I heard. I'm so sorry, Linzi, it's a terrible mess, isn't it?'

'Yes,' Linzi said. What else was there to say in answer to such a question?

'And poor Ritchie...' Megan watched the way Linzi's body tightened, her face grow paler, tenser. Discreetly she changed the subject, 'But let's talk about you—tell me the truth now, how are you? Really?'

In a burst of honesty, Linzi said, 'Just about surviving,' then wished she hadn't given so much away, and turned to slam down the boot of her car. 'Sorry, but I have to go, I have a lot to do,' she muttered.

Megan had noticed the new suitcases, she gave Linzi another quick, shrewd look. 'Going away?'

Linzi nodded.

'On holiday, or for good?'

'For good,' Linzi said shortly.

'When are you leaving? Maybe we could have lunch...'

Shaking her head, Linzi said, 'I'm going later today, I'm afraid. I must rush back to pack, now, Megan—sorry.'

'I heard you'd sent in your notice; Ted mentioned it,' Megan said as Linzi got behind the wheel of her car.

'How is Ted?' Linzi asked, frowning as she remembered the accident, the shock it had given her to see Ted lying there, on his face, his body ominously still. In her nightmares in hospital sometimes the two scenes had blurred and converged, become one—Ted one minute, Barty the next, a repeating pattern of fear and death with herself and Ritchie the connecting threads.

Megan smiled warmly. 'Oh, he's OK now, and, touch wood, there'll be no after-effects from the head injury; even the headaches have stopped. Back at work this week, in fact. He's tough, my Ted.'

Linzi managed a smile. 'Yes, thank heavens. Well, give him my love. I must rush; sorry. Bye, Megan.' Then she started the engine, and Megan stood on the pavement and watched her drive away.

The flat was very neat and tidy. Aunt Ella had spent two days putting it into spick and span order; all Linzi had to do was pack up those possessions she was taking with her and stack everything else into some empty cartons to be stored by a removal firm until she'd decided what she wanted to do with them. She and Barty had had a long lease on the flat; an estate agent was going to try to sell the lea.e, so she wanted the flat cleared.

A few hours later, she was ready to leave. She put the last box into the car and paused on her way back to look around her. She had lived here for several years: mostly painful ones. Leaving it was a peculiar wrench yet at the same time she couldn't wait to get away, she couldn't bear to be here.

Her eyes dwelt on the trees in the garden: already there were a few golden leaves among the green. She had only been in hospital for two weeks, yet autumn was inexorably approaching. Melancholy invaded her. Nothing lasted, did it? Not summer, not happiness, not life itself.

She shook herself free and ran back to lock up the flat, then went back to her car. Before she reached it another car pulled up behind it and with a blinding shock she saw Ritchie leap out.

Linzi ran towards her own car but he was in her path; forcing her to stop.

She couldn't look at him for a second then she threw back her head, her silvery hair flying back from her pale face as an autumn wind suddenly blew, and met his hard eyes with a convulsion of emotions—fear and bitter anger, guilt and pain.

'I thought the police had arrested you!'

'I'm out on bail.' His voice was curt; the sound of it sent a shudder down her spine. From the first moment she met him she had felt this instinctive physical response and been frightened, ashamed of it; now it made her sick to be forced to admit he still got to her like that. She hated herself for feeling her stomach churn, her blood run faster, just because he was close to her. Did she really have to remind herself that he had killed Barty? Guilt ate into her like a corrosive acid; her soul withered.

'I don't ever want to see you again!' she whispered.

He put a hand out to her in an almost pleading gesture, and she struck it away.

'Don't touch me!'

His eyes darkened; glittering pupils, black, obsidian, volcanic, flashed down at her. 'Everything I did was for you! Don't walk away from me now, Linzi!'

Her body flinched as if he'd hit her. 'For me? You killed Barty for me? Do you really think I wanted him dead? I loved him!'

Ritchie's face whitened and stiffened. 'You may have done, once, but he had been hurting you for a long time;

sooner or later he was going to kill you—you knew that, didn't you? I know you did, Linzi. A blind man would have noticed how scared you were. I'd been worried sick about you for weeks…the bruises, the look in your eyes, the way you jumped when anyone came near you.'

She didn't want to remember the fear that had been her constant companion during the last year, but she couldn't let him talk about Barty that way. He would go into court and say these things and the whole world would believe that Barty had been crazy, or vicious, or cruel, and it wasn't true.

'Nothing is that simple! You make it sound so horrible——'

'Well, isn't it? When a man hits a woman like that——'

'You just don't understand!' she burst out. 'Barty loved me! He was unhappy, and sick; he never meant to hurt me. Sometimes things got too much for him and he lost control. It was like an electrical storm breaking out inside him. You could see it in his eyes—the violence, the rage, exploding in his head. We were going to be so happy until he had that accident and we lost everything—our lives just blew up in our faces and Barty had no hope, not any more. There was never going to be a baby, he hated his job, he was in constant pain, and I——'

She broke off and Ritchie watched her intently, his face sombre, eyes quick and alert to pick up every nuance in her voice, her quivering features.

'And you, Linzi?' he whispered. 'He knew you didn't love him any more, didn't he? That was why he was so violent.'

Her skin filled with scalding colour, then blanched again. Her breath hurt in her lungs.

'No,' she said hoarsely. 'That's a lie, I did love him. I loved Barty, I always loved him.'

'Do you have to say it three times to make yourself believe it?' Ritchie asked drily.

Guilt and rage rushed through her. Her hand came up to hit him and Ritchie caught it, drew it down against him, pressing it to his chest, so that she felt the heat of his body through his white shirt, through her own skin and began to shake wildly.

'Let go of me!'

He didn't. He just moved closer, speaking very quietly. 'You may have loved him once, but as you just said your lives had blown up in your faces. He wasn't the man you married. He frightened you. You can't love someone who terrifies you like that. Love and that sort of fear don't co-exist, Linzi. I used to hear you talking to him on the phone; you sounded like a scared child, trying to placate him, hoping against hope that he wasn't going to turn nasty. And he must have known how you felt. You lived with him, he must have seen your eyes, heard your voice. He knew, didn't he?'

She couldn't get a word out. It was true, and yet not true; like seeing yourself in a distorting mirror and knowing it was you although the image was so fractured that you couldn't recognise yourself.

Still holding her hand against him, Ritchie said softly, 'And he knew about me, too, didn't he?'

Her body jerked as if a knife had been plunged into it; she staggered backwards, pulling her hand free. 'G...get out of my w...w...way,' she stammered, then on a rush of anger, 'Let me go or I'll start to scream, and you can explain to the police why you're harassing me in the street! You're only on bail, they could still take you back into custody.'

'Sooner or later you're going to have to face it, Linzi!' he said in a low, hurried, husky voice. 'Don't you know how dangerous it is to lock anything this explosive away in some corner of your mind? You can't just pretend it hasn't happened.'

'I don't even know what you're talking about!' she muttered, but she did, of course, and her heart was lanced with pain and guilt.

He stood there looking at her, not touching her, and her body ached and burned; she was trembling so much that she could barely stand. She hated him for trying to make her admit to feelings she wished she had never felt, had tried to suppress as soon as they started, had tried to pull out like weeds, appalled to realise how deep the roots ran, how tenacious of life they were. She hated herself, even more. Barty might be alive today if she hadn't let herself start to feel ...

'One day it will blow up and send you sky-high,' Ritchie whispered.

'I want to get into my car. Please move out of my way,' Linzi said in a dry whisper, looking away from him, away from the piercing insistence of his eyes. He wasn't forcing any admissions out of her, she was armed against him now.

'These things happen—you can't keep on blaming yourself! You're a human being, not a plaster saint,' he said with leashed impatience. 'Linzi, for God's sake, don't walk away from me now. I need you.'

She tensed again, head bent in a movement of vulnerability, uncertainty. Did he have to say that? Need...the word clutched at her, held her there, listening.

Ritchie watched her pale face, the colourless line of her curved, full mouth, the helpless bend of her neck.

Quietly he said, 'The next year is going to be a terrible strain, waiting for the trial, waiting to find out what's going to happen to me. They're only charging me with manslaughter, we hope. The murder charge will probably be dropped before we come to court. I'll plead guilty and take whatever sentence they give me. My lawyers tell me that in these circumstances it could be five or six years, but that I won't have to serve that long; I should get out sooner, with good behaviour.' His face was dark, shadowed. 'Even so, it's a grim prospect. Don't make it harder for me by walking away.'

Her blue eyes were glazed with unshed tears as she looked up at him. 'I'm sorry, I know you did it for me, and that you never meant to kill Barty, but you did...you did...and I can't forgive you...'

White-faced, his eyes fixed on her as if he couldn't believe what she had said, he took a step back, in a reflex movement, breathing thickly, roughly.

'Don't do this to me, Linzi!' It was a cry of anguish, and hurt her, too, piercing her to the heart.

He no longer blocked her access to the car. She couldn't bear any more; she leapt to open the door and almost fell inside. She slammed the door and locked it before Ritchie could get it open again.

'Linzi!' he groaned, hammering on the closed window, wrenching at the door-handle. 'Don't go, don't...'

She was shaking so much that it was hard to start the engine, get the car moving. Ritchie still held on to the door, his face close to the window, although she didn't look, couldn't bear to look. She drove off with him hanging on, calling her, but as the car picked up speed he let go and she put her foot down and shot round the corner.

She had to get away before he could get into his own car and follow her. She didn't want him to know where she was going. Only the police knew, and they had assured Aunt Ella that they would not give her new address to Ritchie's lawyers. All communication with her would be through her own lawyers.

She turned another corner and lost herself in the maze of little streets before she could be sure Ritchie wasn't close behind her. She drew up by the kerb and sat there for five minutes, shaking so violently that she was afraid she might crash if she drove again for a while. Only when she had stopped trembling did she start the car again. She kept looking into her driving mirror, watching the road behind her, but there was no sign of Ritchie's car. She had lost him.

She wished she could believe she had lost him forever, but she still had to go through the trial. At least he couldn't get to her then; he would be in the dock, and there would be too many other people around. But she would still see him, and even if she didn't look at him she would feel him there, in the same room, breathing the same air. It would be torture.

CHAPTER SIX

NEARLY three years later, on a fine spring morning, Linzi was sitting at a desk in the corner of the antiques shop where she worked, watching two American customers who, from what she overheard them saying to each other, had just visited Stratford and were on their way to Warwick Castle. While they browsed Linzi was polishing some of the silver from a display case, a soothing job she enjoyed.

'Hey, look at this, Ralphy,' the wife said eagerly, holding up a Victorian fairing.

'Cute,' he agreed, warily balancing the little china ornament on his large palm, then he looked at the price tag. His eyebrows shot up. 'But it's pricey! Especially as it's so small.'

'But Ralphy, that's the best thing about it—it'll be so easy to pack!'

'I guess it will!' he agreed and turned to ask Linzi, 'What are these things called, miss?'

'A bridal fairing,' Linzi promptly told him, walking over to join them. 'They sold them at fairs in Victorian times; people gave them to brides as wedding presents.'

'Victorian, huh?' The husband surveyed the china solemnly. 'Can you tell me when it was made, exactly?'

'1871,' Linzi supplied. 'We have some others, as you see, but this is the oldest one we have. That's why it's the most expensive.'

'Trust my wife to pick the most expensive one!' complained the husband.

'She's got good taste!' Linzi said, and the wife grinned at her conspiratorially.

'Right. You tell him! Is this locally made, by the way?'

'No, these fairings were all made in Germany, not England, actually.' Honesty compelled her to admit this, although she was afraid that might make them decide not to buy if they were looking for a locally made souvenir.

The young man's tanned face did alter, but only to light up with real enthusiasm. 'No kidding? Well, what do you know? My ancestors came from Germany. We're going there next. Whereabouts in Germany was this made?'

Linzi gave him a brief talk on the subject of the German factory, which was not as famous as some others, and after listening attentively he nodded.

'We'll have it.' He pulled out a credit card from his wallet. 'I guess you take this?'

'We certainly do,' Linzi said gaily, delighted to have made the sale. Five minutes later she saw the Americans to the door, intending to lock up for lunch as soon as they had gone.

'Enjoy the rest of your visit,' she said as they walked away. She was about to go back into the shop when another car driving past swerved violently and almost hit a van coming in the other direction. The squeal of tyres made Linzi and the Americans look round and stare, then Linzi turned pale with shock as she recognised the face of the driver.

Hurriedly closing the door of the shop, she locked and bolted it, and drew down the blind. She snatched up her handbag from a drawer in the desk, and headed for the back of the shop, meaning to escape through the rear garden and go off to lunch. Before she could, however, somebody began banging on the door.

'Linzi, Linzi...let me in! It's Megan!'

She hesitated, torn between a desire to run and the realisation that if she did Megan would probably just come back some other time. Slowly she turned and went back, unbolted the door, opened it.

Megan hadn't changed an inch in three years. They looked at each other in silence for a moment, then Megan said, 'When I saw you it was such a shock, I almost ran into a van coming towards me! It's surprising I recognised you, though! Oh, Linzi, you're very thin—you've lost lots of weight, haven't you? And you're very pale.'

'I'm OK, really. How are you, Megan?' Linzi huskily murmured. 'How's Ted?'

'Ted's fine, we both are!'

'And the children?' asked Linzi, doggedly trying to keep her from mentioning Ritchie.

'They're fine, too. Oh, Linzi...'

'They must have grown a lot,' Linzi said, trying to sound normal and only aware of the shakiness of her voice.

'Kids do that, keep on growing. I sometimes think I do nothing but buy them new shoes,' Megan said, then she groaned and gave Linzi a wry little grimace. 'Oh, this is ridiculous! We can't talk on the doorstep. Look, can I come in and talk, or will you come out and have a bite of lunch with me? You probably know somewhere around here where we can eat—a pub, if nothing else!'

What could Linzi do but agree? They went to the public house down the street—the Yew Tree. Built in the seventeenth century, its ceilings were low, its red-tiled floors had sunk, the windows were tiny and you hit your head on a beam every time you walked through a doorway. The saloon bar was crowded and gloomy, of very irregular size and shape—but they did offer a pretty good ploughman's plate which both Megan and Linzi ordered. It came quickly: large chunks of home-made bread, delicious Cheddar, a mound of home-made pickles, a couple of tomatoes and some lettuce topped with a spring onion.

'Looks good,' Megan said, lifting her glass of local cider to her lips. 'Do you come here for lunch every day? They seemed to know you.'

'I usually eat sandwiches in the back of the shop, but I do sometimes eat here,' admitted Linzi, breaking off a piece of cheese and crumbling it on her plate with nervous fingers. 'What are you doing around here, Megan? Have you been visiting Stratford? Is Ted with you?'

'No, Ted's back home, with the kids. I've been staying with my younger sister, she's just had her second baby, and I've been looking after her little girl, Tracy, until Jenny's up and about again. She lives in Warwick, just down the road from here. My brother-in-law has taken

Tracy to see her mum, in the hospital, so I came out for a drive to get some fresh air and look at the countryside. I couldn't believe my eyes when I saw you in that shop doorway. How long have you been working here?'

'Ever since I left the north. The shop belongs to my godmother; I live in the flat above it.'

'You've been here all along?' said Megan, cutting her cheese into bite-sized pieces. 'We wondered where you'd gone. Ritchie kept asking if anyone had seen you.'

The name hit Linzi like a blow. She had been expecting Megan to mention him, but even so hearing his name did something drastic to her heartbeat. 'I suppose you and Ted kept in touch with... with him?' she murmured huskily. 'How... how is he?'

Megan gave her a frowning look, visibly hesitated, then burst out, 'I don't know if I ought to warn you, but... Linzi, he may be coming out any day now!'

'What?' Linzi's delicate oval face turned chalk-white. In spite of everything that had happened to her she still looked much younger than she was, because of her long, straight, fine hair and childlike build. Thinner than ever, with small, high breasts and narrow hips, she wore jeans and a T-shirt; a stranger might have taken her for a teenager if he passed her in the street.

In fact, she was now twenty-seven and a closer look would have revealed the shadows in her blue eyes, the fine lines around eyes and mouth which pain had etched into her skin.

'Ritchie! He's coming out?' she whispered, suddenly so cold that she was shivering convulsively. 'But... he got three years!'

It was a year and a half since she last saw Ritchie Calhoun—in a stuffy courtroom, on a day in early summer, all the windows wide open and a brass fan turning on the ceiling above the well of the court, yet the air still humid, heavy with the scent of white lilac growing outside in the formal garden surrounding the building.

She could remember every detail: she had tried never to think about those days in court yet in her dreams she often found herself back there, reliving the agony of telling all those strangers what had happened, the inner secrets of her private life, things she had never told anyone before. It had been painful to admit to Barty's moods, his drinking, his violence—to talk in open court about her lost baby, Barty's impotence and how he had felt about that. She hadn't wanted to answer many of the questions, but Ritchie's defence counsel had forced the answers out of her.

She had kept her eyes fixed on the lawyers questioning her, never moving her gaze towards the man in the dock, except once, early on in her evidence, when she was asked to look at him and identify him.

She had given him a swift, blind look, not meeting his eyes, then looked away. Given a nod. Yes, that was him.

After that she hadn't looked at him again, but throughout that long ordeal she could feel his gaze fixed on her. He had never once looked away. Insistently, relentlessly, he had stared at her, and, despite the heat of the weather she had been icily chill and had kept shivering. Once or twice she had almost fainted; a glass of water had been offered to her, and she had been allowed to sit down to finish her evidence.

She was in court to hear the sentence. Aunt Ella had suggested they leave first, but Linzi had had to stay. She could not have left without knowing what was going to happen to him. When the sentence was announced she had turned paler than the prisoner himself and swayed, her eyes almost closing. Three years in prison! Three years out of his life!

Aunt Ella had taken her out then. As they got up to leave, she had felt Ritchie watching, felt him willing her to look at him. Her eyes had been drawn towards him like a magnet turning to the north. Across the room their eyes had met; she could remember it as if it had happened yesterday, the brass fan whirring overhead, the hushed whispering from the people in the public seats, Ritchie's dark, mesmeric eyes staring into hers, piercing her to the heart.

She had felt the strangest sensation of confusion. The rest of the people in the room had vanished, fallen away. For a moment, she was alone with Ritchie; fixed by his gaze, she was drowning in a rush of guilt, shame and regret; as if she was the one who should be standing in that dock, should be facing punishment. All of this was her fault and Ritchie was being punished in her place.

Aunt Ella had led her out, an arm around her; but Ritchie had gone with her, in her head, and however hard she tried to evict him he had been there, ever since.

She looked at Megan with distraught eyes. 'He's only served eighteen months—they wouldn't release him yet, surely!'

Megan said flatly, 'These days, people don't usually serve their full term, and Ritchie's been a model prisoner. He's up for parole this week and if they grant it he'll be let out at once.'

It hadn't occurred to Linzi that he might get out early; her mouth was ash-dry. She took a long drink of cider, trying to think about the implications of what Megan had told her.

'At once?' she whispered.

Megan nodded. Her voice low, she muttered, 'Linzi, you know as soon as he is out he is going to come looking for you, don't you?'

Linzi's blue eyes dilated, their pupils glittering, black as sloes. 'He won't!'

Megan gave her a wry glance. 'Ted says he's getting a private detective to look for you.'

Linzi's nerves jumped. 'A detective?' She was appalled. 'Megan, don't tell him where I am! Promise you won't, Megan! Don't tell anyone, not even Ted!'

There was disapproval in Megan's face, her voice cooled. 'Don't you think you owe it to Ritchie to see him?'

'I can't!' Linzi said wildly, getting up. 'I'm sorry, but I can't.'

She walked towards the exit and Megan followed her, caught up with her in the busy high street. She put a hand on Linzi's arm, forcing her to stop as she hurried along the pavement.

'I won't tell him, if you don't want me to!' she promised, and Linzi relaxed. Watching her face, Megan sighed, 'But I'm warning you, Ted says Ritchie is obsessed with finding you, I don't think he'll stop looking until he does. Linzi, he has paid a terrible price for trying to save your life...why won't you see him?'

Linzi looked at her with disbelief. 'Isn't it obvious? Whatever the reason...he killed my husband! Do you really expect me to shrug and say, ''Well, let bygones be bygones''?'

'It was almost an accident, though!' protested Megan. 'And if it hadn't been for you, Ritchie would have spent the last two years as a free man. Ted says he's changed a lot. He was always quite tough, but now he's hard, almost bitter. Prison hasn't been easy for him.'

Linzi bent her head, her fine hair flowing down against her pale skin. 'No, I don't suppose it was.'

They walked along towards the antiques shop and halted outside. Megan gave her a sideways look, then tentatively said, 'Ted thinks Ritchie's angry because you gave evidence against him...'

'I had to!'

'I know, but he seemed to feel you had turned against him. You never visited him, wouldn't see him, you disappeared and nobody knew where you'd gone. Over the months while Ted's been visiting him, Ritchie has changed, grown very moody. He talks about you a lot, Ted think he broods over you when he's alone, that he was expecting you to visit him in prison, stand by him. He took it badly when you went away.'

There was the echo of a question mark against the last remark. Linzi sensed a dammed-up curiosity in Megan. It didn't surprise her. During the trial it had been only too clear that many people thought there was a lot that hadn't come out, hadn't been said. People had stared at her, whispered, everywhere she went, wondering exactly what her relationship with Ritchie had been, whether they had been secret lovers, whether her husband had found out, whether that was why he had attacked her, why Ritchie had killed him.

During the days of the trial she had been followed everywhere by reporters; flashlights exploding in her face as she walked along streets, men trying to grab her, jostling around her, firing off questions that made her wince and flush and tremble. They had had no pity; her obvious shock and dismay had only made them pursue her the more relentlessly, like sharks scenting blood.

Hints had been dropped to her by reporters, slyly implying that she and Ritchie might have wanted Barty dead, out of their way. Nobody had dared print that, for fear of a libel suit, but Linzi had not been left in any doubt about the gossip and innuendo circulating. Nobody seemed to want to believe that there had been no love-affair between her and Ritchie, and she had resented that, she still did.

Sometimes she shook with anger when she thought about some of the things people had said.

One reporter had actually told her, 'People will say there's no smoke without fire, you know. Talk to me and I'll put your side of it!' And the worst part of that was that although she had never had an affair with Ritchie there was still a spark hidden in all that smoke. In a way that made it harder. She had fought her secret attraction towards Ritchie and won—but she had still been condemned for it, punished for it. That was what was so bitterly unfair.

'Visit him?' she said fiercely now, to Megan. 'Me, visit him in prison? If he thought I would, he's out of his mind. He killed Barty!'

'But he didn't mean to, Linzi!' Megan said earnestly. 'He was trying to save your life! He walked in and saw your husband strangling you and just picked up the nearest thing and hit him with it. It was a reflex action. An accident, almost. He didn't intend to kill Barty!'

'But he did!' Linzi muttered. 'Oh, I know what you all thought! But it wasn't true, there was nothing between me and Ritchie Calhoun. I just worked for him. We were never lovers. I loved my husband, and Ritchie killed him! Visit him in prison? I never want to see him again!'

'That's very unfair,' Megan protested indignantly. 'Poor Ritchie, aren't you sorry for him? After all he's gone through? He's a wonderful boss and a good friend, and let me tell you...I never believed all that gossip about you and Ritchie in the first place! I know both of you, and I knew it was lies. I know how loyal you were to your husband. I remember the way he got drunk at our party. Everyone knew he was a drinker, and felt sorry for you, but I saw you were still very fond of your husband. But honestly, Linzi! Being faithful is one thing—pretending he wasn't actually trying to kill you is behaving like an ostrich.'

'No!' Linzi put her hands over her ears to shut out the quiet voice.

'Linzi, the medical evidence was too strong—you can't deny it!'

'Barty grabbed me by the throat, but he wouldn't have killed me, he'd have stopped of his own accord, he always had before! Ritchie didn't need to hit him so hard!'

Megan made a soft sound of horror and pity. 'He always had before? My God, Linzi, how often had it happened? How often had he almost killed you? And you go on saying he loved you!'

Her small face stubborn, Linzi huskily said, 'Barty loved me, Megan. If you'd only known him when we were young! He was warm and tender and loving, a wonderful friend, great fun to be with, and a wonderful husband, too. Then all that changed after his accident. OK, he could be violent, at times I think he almost hated me, because I was fine and his life had been blasted— but I never doubted that underneath all that, he still loved me.'

Megan had listened intently. 'You're very loyal, and I admire that,' she slowly said. 'I hope I'd be as loyal to my Ted, if it happened to us, God forbid. OK, I won't say another word. But Ritchie is going to keep looking until he finds you, dear, so if you really don't want to see him again perhaps you had better move on? Because from what Ted says this obsession of his is worrying. I wouldn't want you to get hurt again.'

Linzi gave her a wide-eyed, shaken look.

Megan shrugged. 'Think about it.' She glanced at her watch. 'I'd better go; I have to be back before my brother-in-law gets back from the hospital. Look, give me your phone number. I'll get in touch the minute I have any news.'

'Thank you, Megan,' Linzi said huskily.

Megan gave her a warm hug and then she was gone. Linzi walked slowly back to the antiques shop, her brain buzzing with shock. Ritchie might soon be out of prison—a free man again. But she wouldn't be free. She had been in prison ever since the day Barty was killed, shut out of life, behind bars nobody could see, and she was still imprisoned, without hope of a parole.

The events of that night three years ago had marked her in many different ways; most of them invisible to others.

She closed her eyes, a groan wrenching her as she unlocked the door of the shop and opened up again although there were no customers around. People would still be eating their lunch.

A while later she was walking around the shop, picking up antiques, staring at others, trying to think clearly. Was it really nearly three years since Barty died, eighteen months since Ritchie was sent to prison? The time had gone by so fast.

What had she done since she'd left the north? Nothing, just existed, like a buried seed in the dark, waiting for a chance to break out to the light. The years had gone by without her counting the days.

Now Ritchie would soon be free. Free to come looking for her! Panic made her nerves flash like electric sparks; she had trouble breathing. Was Megan right? Would he want to see her? After all this time? It was so long since they'd seen each other—surely he would have forgotten all about her?

Have you forgotten about him? asked a chill little voice inside her, and Linzi knew she hadn't; how could she?

She wished she could. She had tried hard enough, heaven knew. She would have thought he would want to forget, too. Surely it must have been a nightmare for him, too, one he wanted just to put behind him?

Then she remembered the way he had looked at her in that courtroom. That strange intensity that made her heart stop, that had left her barely able to walk, she was trembling so much.

Even remembering it could make her heart miss a beat, and she had dreamt about that moment night after night; it had haunted her. But could she help the way her unconscious dealt with the turmoil of the past? You couldn't take any notice of dreams, they were a snare and a delusion. They didn't mean anything.

Why are you lying to yourself? she thought then, biting her lip. You know what those dreams were about. Ritchie had known, he had challenged her directly, tried to make her admit how she felt, but had failed.

She couldn't admit anything.

Her secret emotions were a snake lying coiled in the very depths of her mind. Every time she caught sight of it she fled. The guilt she felt over Barty's death was all mixed up with guilt over Ritchie; a secret dread that when Ritchie hit out at Barty he had half wanted to kill him, a dread too that she had wanted Barty out of her life, that she had wanted it all to end.

Oh, God, stop thinking! she told herself, pausing in her restless pacing of the shop, in front of a long-case clock which Aunt Ella's son, Gareth, was working on at the moment. She stared at that, made herself think about it, about Gareth.

Gareth was good with clocks and watches, and if the problem was too complicated for him they got somebody more expert to deal with it. This clock had a wonderful case; marquetry made it shine in the sunlight as if the wood were jewelled. Linzi loved the painted face, too; the elegant iron arrows which were the clock hands pointed to two o'clock. Surprised to see it was only that time, she frowned—where was Aunt Ella? She should be back by now.

A moment later someone hurried into the shop—a big, fair man in jeans and a black T-shirt, carrying a large box in his arms, who grinned cheerfully at her.

'Mum did well at the auction. We managed to get some good stuff very cheap—there weren't many dealers there, they'd all gone over to the big sale at Grenoch Hall, hoping to pick up some of the Grenoch porcelain and glass collection.' He put the box on the shop counter and peered into it, not yet noticing Linzi's pallor, the look of shock in her eyes. 'Very nice silver dressing-table set. Tarnished, but we'll soon make it shine again. Some silver photo frames; mostly twentieth century. And what do you think of this?'

He fished out a small hand mirror set in an ormolu frame, and she took it from him.

'It's lovely,' she murmured.

'Isn't it? But does it say Art Nouveau to you? Mum swears it is, but there's no provenance, no date on it, and we couldn't find the maker's name. I had a feeling it could be a later reproduction.'

With a faintly unsteady finger, Linzi traced the sinuous, curving lines of the design. 'Could be, but this has the right feel. I've seen something like this before, Austrian, I think, a Viennese manufacturer. Definitely not English.'

Gareth nodded, taking her opinion seriously. Linzi had picked up a good deal about antiques during the two years she had worked in the shop.

'That's what Mum said.'

Aunt Ella had lent Linzi lots of books on antiques, and talked to her constantly about what came into the shop, what they saw on visits to museums and art galleries all around Britain. Linzi had taken evening classes, had taken to dropping in on other shops to browse and explore and ask questions, sometimes even buy the odd item.

She didn't have much money to spare, but she was collecting tiny objects which she kept in a case in her flat. What had simply been a job for her, in the beginning, had become Linzi's hobby and then a passion.

It was a passion shared by Aunt Ella and Gareth, too; selling and buying antiques was their business but it meant far more than that.

Gareth was seven years older than Linzi, but where she looked younger than her age Gareth looked far older. The death of his wife had aged him prematurely, carved lines into his forehead and around eyes and mouth, put sadness into his deep-set blue eyes. Linzi knew he still grieved for her. His little boy, Paul, who was now nine years old, had got over his mother's death far better. He loved his grandmother; she gave him a stability and sense of security he needed. If he still missed his mother he didn't show it. He seemed very lively and cheerful.

Linzi understood Gareth very well. She and Gareth were so much alike that people often took them for brother and sister. They shared the same colouring, the same blue-eyed stare, the same way of smiling; but Gareth was a big, powerfully built man, with strong, very masculine features, and a determined nature, fuelled by ambition and energy. Since his wife's death he had given most of his attention to building up his own business, a large garage on the outskirts of Stratford. From time to time he helped his mother in the shop, and he enjoyed going to auctions with her, but his leisure was exclusively devoted to his son. Gareth was a warm-hearted, loving father, but in the centre of his life there was a black hole. He had not stopped grieving for his wife in all this time; perhaps he never would. He was stubbornly faithful to her, and if they all went out to see a film, or to dinner, or were just having fun together in the shop, laughing and talking, Gareth would some-times stop short, frown, look guilty, as though he had no right to be happy any more. And in that, too, there was a likeness to Linzi.

Grief had been her constant companion too, for the past three years. Grief and guilt.

'Who do we know who's an Art Nouveau expert?' Gareth took the mirror back from her and studied it.

'It does look right, doesn't it?' Without looking up he asked, 'What sort of morning did you have, anyway? Sell anything?'

'Some of the Dutch tiles, a set of silver spoons, and one of the Victorian fairings,' she slowly said, recollecting the sales with difficulty because what Megan had told her had blotted out everything else that had happened that day.

'Not bad at all!' Gareth said. 'Well done, girl!' The door was pushed open, the bell chimed, and Gareth put down the mirror and hurried to help his mother with the box she was carrying. 'Linzi thinks you're right about the mirror, Mum, and at a closer look I must say I agree.'

'Of course I'm right,' Aunt Ella said breathlessly and sank down on to a balloon-back Victorian chair with plum-coloured velvet upholstering that wasn't original but looked it. If people didn't ask, they didn't point that out, but they never lied about such things. That was Ella Killian's decision. She liked, she said, to be able to sleep at nights, not stay up brooding over cheating people.

'My word, that brass is heavy,' she said. 'A real bargain, though, Linzi—Edwardian horse-brasses, absolutely genuine, a complete set. Have you got the kettle on? I'm dying for a cup of tea.'

Linzi turned to obey and Aunt Ella gave a little gasp of concern as the light fell on her face. 'Why, Linzi, dear, you look ill—whatever's wrong?'

Gareth looked at Linzi closely, too, his brows pulling together. She looked back at them both, her blue eyes wide and glazed with unshed tears, face drained of colour, her lip trembling.

'What on earth's wrong, Linzi?' Gareth asked, putting a comforting arm round her slender shoulders and hugging her close to him.

'I had a phone call,' she huskily told them. 'Ritchie Calhoun will be released from prison tomorrow morning. I bumped into someone I used to know and she warned me it might happen—then she called me to tell me it was definite.'

Aunt Ella gasped. 'Already?'

Linzi nodded, then, on a rush she added almost desperately, 'I can't stay here. Megan promised not to tell him where I am, but I think she told him I had left the hospital and was moving out of my flat, the last time I saw him. Somebody must have told him he'd find me there! The only one who knew apart from you two was Megan, and I know she's his friend, she's very sympathetic to him. She's nice to me, too, but in the last resort she's on Ritchie's side. I have to get away, before he finds me!'

Ritchie Calhoun walked out of the prison gates and then paused to take a long, slow look at the world he had not seen for two years.

'They always do that,' said the warder who had unlocked the gate for him, to a younger man who had only started to work in the prison that week and was learning the routine.

'You'd have thought they wanted to get as far away as possible before they stop!' the young warder thought aloud.

The older warder didn't answer. He was busy watching the prisoner, who was taking a deep breath, his shoulders going back as he inhaled. It was a cool, hazy morning with a promise of heat later; the sun burnt orange behind an opalescent mist high above the city.

The prisoner stared at the horizon hungrily, free at last to go as far as he liked, seeing everything with the eyes of someone who had not been free for so long that he had forgotten how it felt. He had lost weight and it showed. His expensively tailored dark grey suit no longer fitted the way it had: the jacket was loose, hung on him, the trousers sagged slightly from the waistband.

That wasn't the only visible change in him. There was a silver streak at his temples, among his thick, smooth dark hair, which was not cut very short, close to his head. There hadn't been a trace of grey in his hair three years ago.

His face was pale, the almost grey prison pallor all the men had; no sign now of the habitual tan he had once had when he spent a lot of time out in the fresh air, his skin weathered and sunflushed, especially when he took long holidays abroad, in warmer climates. The bone-structure of his face was even more pronounced, his skin tight and fleshless, over features that had a hardness that was new, too.

'He looks tough,' the young warder said, and the older one laughed.

'Tougher than he was when he came in, anyway! He didn't have an easy time of it at first—he was a bit of a target for some of the hard men. But once they knew he could handle himself they left him alone.'

A long black car was parked near by. The driver, a wiry little man going slightly bald, a livid scar showing on his forehead, had got out and was standing patiently, with the passenger door open beside him, watching the released prisoner.

Suddenly, Ritchie Calhoun caught sight of him; a smile came into his face, he walked over there and held out a hand.

'Thanks for coming, Ted.'

'Good to have you back,' Ted Hobson said, shaking hands, his eyes searching Ritchie's face, noting the spare austerity of the features, the tension of mouth and jaw, the hard glitter of the eyes. 'How are you, Ritchie?' he asked anxiously, trying to sound cheerful. 'You look pretty fit to me. Lost weight, but it suits you.'

'I'm OK.' Ritchie got into the car and Ted slid behind the wheel, started the engine again.

'Megan has cooked something extra-special for lunch; we hoped you'd eat it with us,' he said, uncertainly watching Ritchie in the mirror above his head.

The hard face warmed slightly. 'That's very good of you both, but if you don't mind I'd like to get home. Can I take a rain-check on the lunch? And give my love to Megan. I shall look forward to seeing something of her very soon. But today I want to talk to the detective agency I've been using—they think they may have picked up a new trail, they may have found her.'

Ted's eyes grew more worried. 'Look, I may be speaking out of turn, but I have to say this—don't go looking for her, Ritchie. If you'd never met her, none of it would have happened. Now you're out and you can get on with your life again, put it all behind you. Why don't you be sensible, and just forget you ever met her?'

Ritchie stared out of the window, his face in profile, darkly set, his grey eyes smouldering.

'Forget her? No, Ted.' His voice was low, harsh, barely audible. 'I've been waiting to catch up with her for three years and I'm going to find her if it takes me the rest of my life!'

CHAPTER SEVEN

LINZI was mowing the lawn when she heard a car driving along the unmade road which led to the cottage. Stiffening, she switched off the electric mower and peered through the tall hedge of elder, hawthorn and wild rose, her nerves on edge until she recognised Gareth's car.

He parked, and got a large cardboard box out of the boot, piled high with groceries for her, she was glad to see. She had almost run out of various necessities.

She met Gareth at the gate, opened it for him, leaning over to kiss his cheek. 'Nice to have some company for a change! Isn't it a gorgeous day for early May? What have you brought me?'

'Mum did the shopping.' His eyes searched her face. 'You OK? Not too lonely out here?'

'It's quite peaceful, actually. I'm doing lots of reading and listening to music—I'm not lonely but I do miss you and your mother, and Paul. I wouldn't like to spend too long here. I suppose human beings were meant to be gregarious.'

'Of course they are, and with luck you should be able to come home very soon,' Gareth said cheerfully.

It was Aunt Ella who, typically, had come up with the solution to Linzi's problem: an isolated little cottage on the edge of a Warwickshire wood with no neighbours and only a narrow winding track leading to it. It belonged to a friend of hers who was now living in Florida a lot of the year but who came back for a few months in the summer, when Florida's heat became intolerable for her, and kept her old home in Warwickshire in order to have a base in England. Aunt Ella had rung her in Miami, asked if Linzi could borrow it, and been given a warm response.

'As long as she looks after the place she's welcome to stay as long as she likes, rent free. I'll be glad to have the cottage lived in for a while. I don't like taking tenants normally, because when I have, in the past, they've made off with everything portable, but I know I can trust someone from your family, Ella!'

Megan had rung a few days later to warn that Ritchie had definitely been released, and Linzi had moved immediately to the cottage.

'I haven't told him I've seen you,' Megan assured her on the phone, but Linzi had been gently sceptical. She knew Megan.

'You didn't tell Ted either?'

Megan had sounded defiant. 'I'm sorry, I know you asked me not to, but I just can't keep secrets from Ted, Linzi. He trusts me; I'd feel guilty if I kept something from him. But I made him promise not to tell Ritchie, so don't worry.'

Linzi had sighed. How long would Ted keep that promise if Ritchie was serious about wanting to find her? Ted was Ritchie's friend; sooner or later he would tell him where she was.

'Well, it doesn't matter, as it happens, because I'm going away,' she told Megan deliberately. 'Aunt Ella has this friend in Florida, who is renting me a place—I rather fancy a trip there. I need a holiday, and I'll be able to get in lots of sunbathing and just lying around relaxing.'

She hadn't needed to lie directly, just not tell the whole truth, and do so in a way that confused and deceived.

'Good,' Megan said, sounding relieved. 'I'm sure you'll have a terrific time in Florida; we went there once, to visit Disney World with the kids. How long will you stay there?'

'Not sure yet. I won't come back here, though. I'll have to find somewhere else to live after my trip.'

Having laid a false trail with Megan, Linzi had packed her car with clothes and food, and driven the half a dozen miles from Rushmere to the isolated little seventeenth-century black and white timbered cottage which was to be her home until she was sure Ritchie had stopped looking for her. Aunt Ella had driven there too, in her own car, to help Linzi settle in, after they had collected the key from the estate agent who looked after the house on the owner's behalf while she was abroad.

That had been a week ago. Linzi had eaten most of the food she had brought originally. She hadn't been able to ring Aunt Ella to ask for new supplies because the cottage had no phone, but she hadn't been worried. If she ran out of food completely she could always drive to a nearby village, but in family conference it had been decided that she would stay out of sight, not go out unless it was absolutely necessary, so she had been expecting a visit from either Aunt Ella or Gareth very soon.

He carried the box of groceries through to the big kitchen which took up half the floor space on the ground floor. The only other room was a big sitting-room which had been created out of several very small rooms; that had chintz curtains and upholstery on comfortable, traditional English armchairs, a bookcase full of books she was reading her way through, and a big fireplace in which, on chilly nights, she was burning logs stacked in a shed beside the cottage. At this time of year the days could be warm, but once the sun went down so did the temperature. The kitchen had pine fittings, an electric hob, oven and microwave, and a big pine table and chairs in an alcove at one end of the room serving as a dining-room.

Gareth had never been there before. Putting the box on the table, he looked around. 'Not bad, is it?'

'I like it.' Linzi had put on the kettle for tea. She began taking stuff out of the box. 'Oh, coffee, thank heavens! I was out of it! Teabags, long-life milk—I was down to my last pint of that...marmalade, my favourite brand...you and Aunt Ella are so thoughtful!'

Gareth helped her begin to put things away. Quietly he said, 'He came, Linzi.'

She froze, her face going stiff and white. 'Himself? When?' Her voice croaked as if her throat was rusty and she felt Gareth watching her, frowning.

'Yesterday. We gave him the story we agreed on...I think he bought it.'

The kettle began to boil. Linzi moved like an automaton to make the tea. 'Are you sure he believed you?' she huskily asked, her hands shaking as she picked up the kettle and poured the boiling water on to the teabags.

Gareth's voice was careful. 'I think so. We said you were in Florida, staying near Disney World; we wouldn't give him the address because you had asked us not to give it to anyone.'

'How did he take that?' she asked with dry lips, wishing Gareth wouldn't keep watching her. She was afraid her face betrayed her; she couldn't stop shaking.

Gareth grimaced. 'Well, let's put it like this...he looked pretty grim! I almost got the feeling he was going to punch me on the nose. He certainly didn't take to me on sight—in fact, he scowled at me. I must say, he's a rather unnerving type, isn't he? I can see why you're worried about seeing him again—he made me nervous, and I don't scare easily. But then I suppose a man capable of killing would be rather alarming. Not many people could kill someone else, could they?'

'Don't talk about it!' Linzi burst out raggedly, and Gareth took a sharp breath, looking horrified.

'I'm sorry, Linzi. Good lord, I could kick myself...I forgot who I was talking to...' He put an arm round her and kissed the top of her head clumsily. 'I'm an idiot.'

She subsided with a sigh, gave him a tremulous, half-apologetic smile. 'No, you didn't mean to hit a nerve, it's me who's sorry—I'd no business yelling at you like that! I ought to be able to talk about it; it is three years now, after all. Oh, sit down, Gareth, have your tea and one of those delicious-looking shortbread biscuits you've brought me.'

Gareth sat down at the pine table and Linzi handed him his cup of tea, and a plate of shortbread.

Gareth inhaled the delicate fragrance of his tea. 'Mmm . . . just what I need . . .' He took a biscuit and bit into it. 'These are nice—try one yourself. Anyway, I think you can start looking forward to leaving here, Linzi. I reckon Ritchie Calhoun will be on his way to Florida by now. Mind you, I kept my eyes peeled while I was coming here, to make sure he wasn't hanging around near the house, or following me. But there was no sign of him. So give it a few more days and then you can risk coming back.'

Linzi nodded; she was not yet ready to feel safe, though. 'I'll see. How's the shop? What have you sold since I left?'

'The long-case clock,' Gareth said, half triumphant, half sad. 'It went for five hundred more than we paid for it, so that was a good profit.'

'But you'll miss it,' Linzi said sympathetically. 'You spent weeks working on that clock!'

Gareth grimaced. 'Yes, but never mind—I bought a very interesting watch yesterday, Swiss, late nineteenth, never seen one like it before. I'm going to have to do lots of research before I touch it. The winding mechanism is broken, but I think I can mend it.'

He drank his tea, looked at the kitchen clock. 'I'm afraid I'll have to go, Linzi. I have to get back to take over from Mum; she's going to see an old man who wants to sell a collection of nineteenth-century miniatures, mostly portraits, a few paintings of houses.'

Linzi saw him to the gate, and before he left gave him a warm hug and a kiss. 'Thanks for coming, Gareth.'

He held her with one arm around her waist, smiling down at her. 'You're welcome, sweetheart. What are cousins for?'

'I'm very lucky to have you and Aunt Ella, I know that. Give her my love and tell her I'm very grateful for all the trouble you've both gone to for me.'

'Look after yourself. It would probably be safe for you to go out more now, but stay in this area, don't go into Stratford or Warwick, just in case he's still hanging around.'

Gareth drove off and Linzi watched him go before going back to her mowing. When she had finished she went indoors, had a shower, put on a sunny yellow bikini top which left her midriff bare, and matching yellow shorts which ended high up on her thigh, exposing long, slim legs beginning to take on a smooth tan. She had been able to do some sunbathing every day she had been here because they were having a burst of very warm weather, unusual in May in England. She collected a historical saga she was reading, her Walkman and a selection of cassette tapes, and went into the garden to sunbathe on a lounger. Before she settled down, she carefully smoothed suntan oil into those parts of her which were exposed to the sun, slid dark glasses on to her nose, put on her headphones, then lay back with a sigh.

She was playing a compilation tape of her own mixing on her Walkman: her favourite songs by top groups. The music surged in her ears and she half listened while she tried to read.

She didn't have any concentration. She kept remembering what Gareth had told her, the story of her book driven out of her head. She stared at some late bluebells showing among the trees in the wood like a blue mist. Would Ritchie follow the false trail to Florida? Surely he wouldn't bother?

Why did it still make her stomach cramp with fierce excitement every time his image came into her mind?

Oh, stop thinking about him, then! she told herself, looking back at her book.

A shadow suddenly fell across the page. With a sharp indrawn breath she looked up, fear in her blue eyes.

'Ritchie!'

For a second she didn't believe he was real. She had dreamt about him so often lately—hot, erotic dreams which made her twist restlessly in her bed. Was this another one? A crazy daydream, her unconscious conjuring up what she most wanted, most dreaded?

Ritchie was looking into the sun; he tilted back his head to look at her through his black lashes, his grey eyes hard and glittering as they roved over her sprawled body on the lounger, the brief bikini top which showed so much of her firm breasts, the smooth skin of her midriff, the long bare legs.

He was no dream, day or night variety. He was real; it was Ritchie standing there a foot away from her.

For three years she had lived with the fear of seeing him again. Now he was here, and her throat closed in panic.

She leapt to her feet to run back into the cottage. Before she had taken a step Ritchie's hand closed round her arm and tethered her. He looked down at her lazily, his mouth twisting.

'Where do you think you're going?'

She stared up at him in dazed confusion, a nerve beating against her mouth. 'Let go of me!'

He laughed and her blood ran cold. He had changed, beyond belief; this was a very different man. Harder, his face honed to razor sharpness, older, a touch of silver at his temples which hadn't been there before, a look in his eyes that terrified.

He was wearing black jeans, a thin pale blue cashmere sweater which left his throat bare and clung to his muscled chest, made it obvious that he was wearing nothing underneath it. She could see every contour of his lean body and looked away, swallowing.

'How did you...?' she whispered and he gave her an icy little smile.

'Find you? Simple. I had a detective trailing your boyfriend.'

'Gareth isn't my boyfriend! He's my cousin.'

'My detective took a picture of the two of you kissing,' Ritchie told her coldly.

She hated the thought of someone secretly watching them, filming them, and her face flushed defiantly. 'I kissed his cheek! So what? Cousins do kiss! I'm fond of him!'

Ritchie sat up slightly, pulled a Polaroid snapshot out of his jeans pocket, looked at it, shrugged, held it up for her to see.

'I believe you, that's a very insipid kiss. Don't ever get fond of me.' He threw the snapshot away; the breeze took it and blew it over the hedge. Arched over her, he looked down at her again, with hard, insolent eyes. 'I want a lot more than an insipid kiss.'

Stiffening, she tried to outstare him. 'You shouldn't have come here! I don't know the terms of your parole, but I think you could get into trouble for bothering me, so go away, now, before I call the police!'

He laughed without humour. 'And how will you do that? You have no neighbours, you don't have a phone!'

She bit her lip. How had he known that? He read the question in her face and drily told her.

'My private detective did some checking. I know who owns this cottage, that she's the one in Florida, that your family lied to me when I visited them.' His mouth twisted. 'They looked me straight in the eye and lied like experts.'

She refused to apologise for that. 'They did it to protect me!'

His face was harsh. 'They're right, you need protection!' he agreed in a voice like the lash of a whip. 'But they aren't here to give it, are they? We're all alone here, Linzi.'

Fear made her flinch and he saw it in her face. His eyes brooded on her for a second, and she really began to get scared then because he wasn't the man she had worked for all those months. Something disastrous had happened to him in the three years since they'd last met. There was a darkness in his eyes: he had lost the veneer of civilisation; everything about him carried an aura of menace, almost of savagery. If it came to a fight between them she wouldn't have a chance against him, and the cottage was so isolated. There wasn't a soul within earshot. She was at his mercy.

Her stomach clenched with a volcanic mixture of fear and excitement.

'I've waited three years to catch up with you,' he whispered, watching her so intently that she felt he knew what she was thinking, could pick up all her feelings.

Her panic grew worse. If he could read her mind she had no privacy from him; if he had the key to her most secret thoughts, how could she protect herself?

'Three bad years, Linzi,' he said curtly. 'Night and day I've thought of nothing else but you—catching up with you, finally having you...'

She was scarlet. 'Don't say things like that! Ritchie, you...you wouldn't...'

His gaze held her eyes; the blackness of night in his stare. 'I would,' he whispered. 'I will.'

'Don't threaten me!' she whispered hoarsely, shaking and knowing that he could feel the tremors running through her body. She fought to control them but her body was out of her control.

'Threaten you?' He smiled coldly. 'That isn't a threat, Linzi, it's a simple statement of fact. An army couldn't stop me taking you now. Three years ago, I needed you, I begged you to stand by me, and you walked out on me.'

'I didn't have any choice!' she said, anguished. 'After you killed Barty, how could I ever see you again?'

His hand tightening on her arm, he bent angrily towards her, and she flinched, stiffening.

Ritchie froze too, his grey eyes glittering like black stars.

'What did you think I was going to do?' he bit out, ice on his voice. 'Kill you too?'

Shock made her eyes dilate; she hadn't known what he might do. This man was a stranger: unpredictable, disturbing. She couldn't begin to guess what he might do to her but he frightened her.

He laughed bitterly. 'Oh, don't worry,' he drawled. 'That wasn't what I had in mind. Although the idea has occurred to me once or twice! When I was in that place, spending a lot of my time locked up in a cell hardly bigger than a broom cupboard, I used to fantasise about what I'd do to you when I caught up with you.' He gave her a cold, mocking smile. 'But killing you wasn't often an option. No, Linzi, I had other plans for you.'

And then he swooped. His head came down so suddenly that Linzi didn't know what was happening until too late. She cried out in shock as his mouth touched her, the moist warmth of his tongue moving sensuously between her startled, parted lips.

She began to shake so violently she couldn't stand up. Ritchie took hold of her shoulders, still kissing her; she hung between his hands like a limp rag doll.

A second later he had taken his mouth off hers and she found herself tumbling back on to the lounger. Her long, fine hair blew across her face, blinding her. Before she could get up, Ritchie was on top of her, the weight of his body knocking all the breath out of her for that instant.

'No, don't,' she muttered, her hands pushing at his wide shoulders, struggling underneath him.

His hands caressed her bare midriff, trailing slowly across her smooth skin, his fingertips cool, tormenting.

'This is what I dreamt about for three years,' he whispered, kissing her throat, light, flickering, frustratingly brief kisses brushing upwards, under her chin, behind her ears, along her jawline.

She was shuddering, her mouth parted, breathing so fast that it hurt as she felt his hand creeping upwards to touch her breast.

She jack-knifed in panic then, her hands clenching into fists. 'Stop it now, Ritchie! Stop...'

He lifted his head, his hand splayed against the full curve of her breast under the thin, silky bikini top.

'What did you dream about all those years, Linzi?' He was smiling, but there was cruelty in the hard line of his mouth. Megan had been right: Ritchie was bitterly angry with her for leaving him to take the full force of the law alone.

She told herself she didn't need to feel any guilt or regret—how could she have done anything else? Yet guilt and regret had been with her ever since the day it happened. He might have been the one who hit Barty, but she had blamed herself, far more than she blamed him. In a twisted way she had been punishing herself for Barty's death by walking away from Ritchie. She had shut herself into a prison of unhappiness and frustration.

Ritchie's other hand was somehow imprisoned underneath her; wriggling. She couldn't work out what he was doing for a second, then she heard something snap and felt her bikini top give.

Before she could grab it and hold it up, the silky scrap of material slithered down. She felt the sun on her bare flesh and Ritchie propped himself up on his elbows, staring down at her.

'You're even lovelier than you were three years ago,' he said thickly, and her heart missed a beat.

He groaned and suddenly he was burrowing between her naked breasts, his lips urgent, heated. She fought not to feel the full sensual intensity of what he was doing, but it was years since a man had made love to her, and needles of sexual excitement had begun to pierce her whole body.

Part of her ached to stop fighting, abandon herself to this intense desire, but she couldn't. Guilt and shame chained her.

She half sobbed, 'Ritchie, I'll hate you if you go on, stop it now, stop it, let me go!'

His head lifted again; he looked down at her, his mouth parted, his breathing ragged, his face darkly flushed.

'Hate me, then,' he muttered. 'I don't give a damn whether you call it love or hate, so long as what you feel is violent, and don't tell me it isn't, because I can feel it, Linzi. You want me as much as I want you.'

She felt as if he had punched her in the stomach. Her body jerked, stiff as rigor mortis.

He knew. She wasn't hiding anything from him, after all. He knew what was happening inside her, this wild need, this clamouring ache. She looked away, shaking her head without hoping to convince him he was wrong.

'I don't!'

'Liar,' he threw back at her, his face hard, contemptuous. 'You want me, Linzi. Who are you really lying to, me or yourself? Stop being such a coward. Admit it!'

'There's nothing to admit!'

His mouth was crooked. 'It was there between us from the very first day, when you walked into my office. I knew it at first sight, although I wasn't ready for a long time to admit what had happened to me. I'd made up my mind to have a middle-aged, safely married secretary, someone who wouldn't cause any trouble or try to get our relationship on to a personal level—then you walked in, far too lovely, far too young, and the minute I saw you I was lost. I was lying to myself then. I made up all sorts of specious reasons why I was determined to pick you although you weren't the best-qualified applicant. It was only later that I faced the truth—that I'd simply realised at once that I had to have you; and I am going to have you, Linzi, make no mistake about it.'

'Stop saying that!' There was a raw edge to Linzi's voice and she felt her pulses beating a wild tattoo.

He caught her face in one insistent hand, tilted her chin up, trying to make her look at him. 'No, Linzi! You stop lying! You can't go on living a lie. We've already tried pretending nothing was happening—when you were working for me. It got worse and worse, day by day, didn't it? For both of us. Every time I buzzed for you and you walked in I felt my heart turn over. Every time you looked at me, my mouth went dry. Every time you smiled I was dizzy. I fell deeper and deeper in love as the weeks went by, and I didn't know what to do about it. I wanted you so much at times that I was practically out of my head, and you knew what was happening to me!'

'I didn't!' she lied, her heart banging inside her like a drum.

'Yes,' he said, and kissed her, his tongue-tip touching hers in an intimate contact that made a shiver of sensuality run down her back. The slow, hot movement of his lips made her want to close her eyes, made her desperate to kiss him back, touch him at last, as she had often dreamt of doing. But she couldn't. She mustn't let herself weaken, give in; this was her punishment, not to have the man she loved, never to know the sweetness of satisfied passion. But she couldn't stop trembling, her blood running like wildfire through her veins. She wanted him more than she had ever in her life imagined she could want anything. The struggle between her conscience and her desire exhausted her.

At last, Ritchie reluctantly detached his mouth with a long sigh. She felt him watching her, looking for telltale signs of what his kiss had done to her, and somehow kept her face tight, shuttered.

Don't let him guess what's going on inside you, she warned herself. Don't betray Barty. You owe it to him not to weaken.

'We both knew what was happening to us,' Ritchie said harshly. 'And I knew something was very wrong with your marriage. You weren't happy. You were always so pale, you had a sad look in your eyes. Then I began to notice the bruises, even though you tried to hide them with make-up.'

She kept her eyes down, emptied her face of expression, hid her thoughts from him. She mustn't give Barty away; she had betrayed him once, in that courtroom, and she mustn't do it again. Barty had lost everything, even his life. All her fault. She had no right to be happy any more.

Ritchie made a rough, angry little sound. 'Are you listening to me, Linzi? Do you know how I felt when I realised that that husband of yours was knocking you about? I was frantic. You wouldn't talk about it, wouldn't even admit it happened. I didn't know how serious it was, but I was scared you were going to get badly hurt one day. I tried to get you to open up about it, but you were so obstinate . . .'

'How could I?' she muttered. 'Why should I? It was nothing to do with you! You keep saying you can see inside my head, so why can't you see why I refused to let you get involved? Barty was my husband, and——'

'Don't say you loved him!' he erupted. 'I'm sick of hearing you say that. You may have loved him once, but by the time you came to work for me you had stopped loving him.'

The harshness of his voice made her wince. 'Stop shouting at me!'

'Then stop lying! From now on all I want to hear from you is the truth, the whole truth and nothing but the truth!'

'There's no such thing! Everything doesn't come in black or white—most things are different shades of grey!'

Their eyes fought and Ritchie's mouth was a hard, white line. 'You're trying to confuse the issue, but it won't work, Linzi! You know what I mean! There's no need to lie any more. You can't hurt him any more; if he knows anything then he knows the truth of how you felt, how you feel now. So why lie about it? Can't you see, the punishment is over? We can start again, Linzi. It isn't just me who is out of prison, you are, too. We're both free, the past's behind us, we can forget it.'

She couldn't. She was silenced by her sense of right and wrong, by her awareness of the ghost standing between them, by old loyalties, old love. The past was their enemy, a wall between them. Ritchie had created this unpassable gulf by killing her husband. Couldn't he understand that?

'I loved Barty,' she said obstinately, miserably; and saw the angry flare of Ritchie's eyes, a smouldering jealousy which tightened the angles of his face, made him look barbaric.

'When you married him, maybe! He was your first boyfriend, wasn't he? You were Romeo and Juliet, the boy and girl next door, young love incarnate—oh, I remember everything you said in court, giving evidence.'

The reminder startled her. When she was telling the court about her marriage, she realised, Ritchie had been listening too. He had never taken his eyes from her.

His voice grim, he said, 'It was the first time I'd been able to hear what your life with him had been like, or don't you realise how much of the truth you admitted?'

She was silent. Oh, she realised. But she preferred to forget the ordeal of giving evidence in court, talking about her marriage, allowing strangers to glimpse the hell on earth she had had to suffer.

After a moment, Ritchie said quietly, 'By the time you met me your marriage had died, hadn't it? You can come up with all the excuses you like but the truth is, he wasn't the man you'd married any more. After his accident he was very ill and when he came back he was different. He didn't even love you any more, he almost hated you; that was why he kept beating you up. He resented you because you were still normal, you had good health, you could make love, you could still have babies. He felt he wasn't a real man any more. He couldn't really be your husband, even though he lived under the same roof. He couldn't love you, so he hated you.'

Stung to the heart, she cried out angrily, 'That isn't true! You didn't know him.'

'I think it was you who didn't know him, Linzi,' Ritchie said in a grave, low voice. 'You persisted in seeing him as the boy you married, when he had become a stranger.'

She fell silent, frowning. She had almost burst out with a denial when what he had said sank in and she was struck dumb. It was true. And yet it wasn't. Life was more complicated than that—there was no one answer, no one way of looking at things. Barty had sometimes hated her, resented her, yet at the same time he'd loved her, wanted her to be happy, had felt guilty because he knew he was hurting her, and he had tried to fight it, to stop the drinking and the violent outbursts.

'He was still my husband, and you killed him,' she said in a low, husky, regretful voice. 'I could never forget that, Ritchie, don't you see? Please go away and don't come back, just leave me alone in future.'

He stared down at her fixedly for a moment, and she nervously sensed that he was on the verge of another volcanic explosion, but then his face changed, stiffened into a cold, remote mask. He abruptly got to his feet, ran a hand through his short dark hair, turned on his heels and walked away, across the lawn, towards the gate.

He's going, she thought, dazedly watching him, he's going, and pain burnt along her nerves, made her eyes shimmer with unshed tears.

CHAPTER EIGHT

LINZI scrambled to her feet in a hurry. She had to get to safety before he changed his mind, came back.

Half blinded with her tears, shakily reclasping her bikini top, she ran into the cottage, slamming the door behind her. For a second she leaned on it, the tears streaming down her face, then she pushed home the bolt. She didn't want Ritchie getting in here. She ran to the front door to check that that was locked, and then stumbled upstairs into her bedroom, roughly drying her eyes with the back of her hand.

She opened the window so that she could look down into the garden—there was no sign of Ritchie, he had gone and she couldn't see a car parked in the lane any more.

If he has gone, he'll be back! a little voice warned in her head. The hard, grim man who had come back from prison wouldn't give up that easily.

Unless he believed you, at last! she thought, turning to walk across the room. Had she finally convinced him that she would never forgive him?

In her dressing-table mirror on the other side of the room she caught sight of herself—a sun-flushed, tear-stained face stared back from between tangled webs of pale hair: she looked at it bitterly.

'You fool!' she hurled at it. 'Now you're going to spend the rest of your life regretting letting him go! Haven't you got enough to regret without being stupid enough to let Ritchie walk away from you?'

But that was her punishment, wasn't it? That was the price she was paying for loving him, for betraying Barty. There was always a price to pay for what you did.

Wearily, she walked into the bathroom and stripped off her clothes, dropped them into the wicker washing basket and turned on the shower. She was so hot that perspiration was running down her spine. She walked into the cubicle, under the jet of water with a deep, wrenched sigh, letting the cool, cleansing stream wash over her. If only she could wash away her memories and feelings as easily!

She groped for the soap in the shell fitted into the tiled wall, and began to wash. A moment later, above the noise of the shower, she heard a sound outside the cubicle. She stiffened, her face running with water, her lashes stuck together, turning to look round.

She hadn't imagined hearing something—there was someone in the room. Through the glass of the cubicle door she saw a dark shadow, the shape of a man, and gasped, dropping the soap from nerveless hands.

The door opened. For an instant she was deaf and blind with panic, then her sight cleared and she saw it was Ritchie.

'Oh...God, you scared me!' she angrily breathed, then frowned. 'But...h...how did you get in?'

'You'd left your bedroom window open. I found a ladder in the garden shed.'

For a split-second she almost felt relief—it could have been worse, it could have been some stranger. She could have been facing rape, or murder. How could she have been such a fool as to leave her bedroom window open?

Then fear and shock of a different sort beat up inside her as she realised the way Ritchie was staring at her. That was when she really began to shake.

'Get out!' she breathed. 'Get out of here! You had no right, climbing in through the window, that's breaking and entering! I'll call the police . . . I'll scream . . .'

His eyes were riveted on her wet, naked body. He was darkly flushed and breathing as if he were dying.

A wave of searing heat swept over her, up her whole body to her face. No man had ever looked at her like that. For the first time she really felt the full force of the desire between them. She stood under cool water and felt as if she were in a furnace. She was burning up and she knew Ritchie was too; she felt the heat coming off him in waves.

'Don't,' she whispered, meaning 'don't look at me like that, don't make me feel like this'.

He didn't bother to answer, just began taking off his sweater in a hurried, deft movement, without looking away from her.

'Stop it!' she yelled. 'Put your sweater back on!' She was beginning to realise that she was trapped, like a fish in a bowl, unable to get out of the cubicle, with him blocking the door. 'Ritchie, what do you think you're doing?' she asked wildly, and it was a stupid question. He gave her a sardonic glance.

She tried not to look, but couldn't take her eyes off him. His body was intensely sexy: beautifully proportioned, very male. His skin still had that prison pallor, and the curling black hair growing in a wedge up the centre of his chest made the pallor more striking by contrast.

Without his sweater on, she could see just how much weight he had actually lost—he had never been overweight, but now he was austerely fleshless, yet still a powerful man, his stomach flat as a board, his midriff taut. As he stretched she saw the muscles in his lean chest, saw muscles ripple in his arm as he hurled his sweater away and began to undo his jeans.

What am I going to do? she asked herself frantically. Oh, pull yourself together! came the impatient answer. Stop staring at him, for a start! And use you head! You've got to get out of here!

She waited until he was standing on one leg, pulling his jeans off the other foot, and then she made a dash for it.

She might have got past him if she hadn't trodden on the soap she had dropped.

Her foot skidded, she slipped sideways with a cry, completely off balance, and would have crashed into the glass if Ritchie hadn't caught her in his arms. She clutched at him wildly and felt a violent shock hit her as their naked bodies collided, hers wet and slippery, his warm and dry.

At that moment she was lost. Her body betrayed her. She gave a long, shuddering moan.

He looked down at her, breathing harshly. 'Got you!' he said in a low, thick whisper, and Linzi felt like someone standing on a beach who felt herself on sand, sinking, unable to hold her ground because it was drifting under her. Ritchie's hand slid down her body, caressed her softly, possessively, in a gesture of ownership that took her breath away.

He suddenly lifted her off her feet, walked forward with her held against him, into the shower, under the jet of water. Only then did he put her down, but he didn't let go of her. He still had his arms around her. His hands slowly fondled her, ran down her back, one following the deep indentation of her spine, making the tiny golden hairs on her peachlike skin stand up, prickling in reaction, the other sensually exploring the warm curve of breast and waist, hip and thigh, smoothly stroking each inch of her.

She had given up pretending. She had given up fighting either him or herself. Her conscience and her sense of guilt were smothered by something more powerful: an elemental drive so strong that she was helpless to stop it once it had her in its grip. She had her eyes closed; she was moaning, shuddering with pleasure. The water ran down their faces as his mouth searched for hers, took it in a slow, intimate possession.

Linzi had to cling to him or fall over; passion was climbing inside her in a tidal wave that was sweeping her away. Her whole body was beating to a hot, persistent rhythm, driving her, clamouring for the satisfaction she had denied it for so long.

Her fingers tightened on Ritchie's long, muscular back as she swayed closer to him, her breasts full and aching, dark-circled nipples hard and erect, pressing into the muscled tension of his chest, his thigh pushing between hers and the water running down between them, around them, trickling through their hair, into their lashes, past their kissing mouths, along all the secret paths of their naked bodies.

His hand clasped her buttocks, pulled her even closer, his fingers exploring lower, between her parting thighs, finding the heat and moisture hidden there; she gave a wild cry and arched against him, her head falling back in utter abandon, her lips apart making those frantic, burning cries.

'Oh, God, I want you,' he whispered, lifting her up.

She had her arms around his neck, let her head tumble down on to his bare, wet shoulder, twined herself around him, her legs around his, her feet touching behind him as he carried her out of the shower cubicle into the bedroom, dripping across the carpet, wet footprints on the pink wool.

Ritchie stripped back the coverlet and sheet in one movement, then lowered her on to the bed. She began to shiver, oddly feverish and chill at the same time, her mouth dry and her teeth chattering in a sort of shock at the force of her own desire. She tried to think, to realise what was happening, but Ritchie didn't give her time to have second thoughts.

His body slid intimately down over her; he found her mouth, his hands busy, too, cupping her breast, wandering in a soft, seductive exploration of her body that lit flames deep inside her.

It was so long since a man had entered her that she felt like a virgin: as he stroked her thighs, sliding between them, she was tense, trembling, fighting him. 'No! Don't...don't hurt me...'

Ritchie lay still, as if listening to that note in her voice, perhaps even understanding her sudden fear. He kissed her softly, coaxingly, their mouths clinging, then his lips slid down her neck, and he kissed her breasts in that slow, tormenting way, until she began to relax again, the tension trickling out of her. She caught his head in both her hands, held it against her, groaning her pleasure, feeling his warm, smooth hair trickling between her trembling fingers, and then Ritchie began to slide downwards, uncoiling on her like a snake, his skin smooth and cool against hers, touching every inch of her, kissing her body as he descended, his head nuzzling her parted white thighs.

Nobody had ever made love to her like that before. Linzi's blue eyes had a startled, confused look as it dawned on her what he was doing. She had often wondered how it felt and now the gentle, sensual incitement of his mouth and tongue sent her into a fierce spiral of climbing pleasure, her body quivering, her cries hoarse. He was driving her crazy, continually breaking off the teasing play of his mouth whenever he felt her coming anywhere near a peak.

She twisted and turned, wordlessly begging him to go on, not to stop, but he did it again, deliberately delaying. Linzi gave a hoarse groan, and wove her fingers angrily into his short, warm hair, tugged, dragging his head up.

He looked at her, his eyes glittering with a wilful triumph, and knew he had won.

'You want me,' he whispered.

Flushed, feverish, she breathed, 'Yes. Ritchie, yes.'

'Say it.'

'I want you, you know I want you.' Now, she thought with an intensity close to anguish; I want him now, at once. The need was absolute. She would have gone through hell fire to have him at that instant; nothing else in the world mattered.

Ritchie's face smouldered darkly, passionately. He stroked her parted thighs, staring down into her face, watching the look in her eyes intently. 'Three years I dreamt of seeing you look like that,' he muttered. 'Night after night, for three long years...'

And then he moved with a fierce intake of breath, and with a shock she felt him entering her. Linzi gave a wild groan, lost to everything from then on but the ending of a sexual tension which was stretched to breaking point. Ritchie was groaning, too, his lean body moving with hers in an erotic rhythm which beat between them like some far-off drum, grew faster and faster, more and more fierce, their skin dry and hot, their faces clenched into masks of rigid desire, primeval, archaic, so that she no longer even knew who was making love to her, she was mindless, lost, abandoned; her body had taken her beyond knowing anything but the race towards a climax that had become a necessity, life or death.

She had never imagined making love could be so sweet or so unbearable. Each movement he made sent ecstatic ripples up inside her body; the pleasure was so intense that it came close to the threshold of pain. She arched towards him, her head falling back and her eyes wide open, her mouth open too, sobbing and moaning as the endless spiral finally became a frenzy. A moment later they reached the pinnacle, together; Linzi heard herself make the sounds of someone being tortured, dying: and that was how it felt. An intense agony engulfed her and Ritchie at the same moment and they clung together, gasping like drowning swimmers, shuddering in the long afterthroes. And yet this agony was at the same time a pleasure so piercing that as the clamouring died down and her body went limp and still she wanted it to begin again.

For a few moments neither of them moved or spoke. They lay on the bed as if they had been knocked down, breathing quickly, eyes closed, heavily flushed.

Then Ritchie rolled over and propped his head up on one hand to stare down at her.

Linzi was overwhelmed with shyness; she couldn't look at him yet. She kept her eyes shut, her long lashes nervously flickering, but she was intensely aware of his gaze. What was he thinking? She wished she knew . . . or did she? It might be better not to know. Men were so bewildering; their minds were difficult to fathom even if you knew them well. She had thought she knew Barty, but she had been wrong. What did she really know of Ritchie? Or of the way he thought?

Her mind flashed her a disconcerting image of herself a couple of minutes ago and her face burned. It was hard to believe that had been her, going crazy on this bed, out of all control.

Was that what Ritchie was thinking about? Was he remembering, too? Oh, God, she thought: how can I ever look him in the face again?

When he started talking she jumped in shock.

'I'll have to be out of here in ten minutes. Ted's flying down to pick me up and take me to London. I'm having dinner with someone important; I have to go. Ted was going to meet me at a local airfield but on the way out here I managed to get in touch with him on my car phone and get him to re-route. He'll put down on the nearest field which looks suitable.' The curt, businesslike tones were like a slap in the face. She couldn't believe he was talking to her like that.

While she was still stunned with the shock of that, Ritchie swung himself off the bed and walked away across the room.

Her hot colour draining away, she opened her eyes to stare after him in disbelief. How could he talk to her in a brusque offhand voice after they had made love like that? She still hadn't stopped shaking after it, yet he seemed to have forgotten already. Hadn't it mean anything to him? The wild intensity, the clamouring need, the long-drawn-out ecstasy, all forgotten?

Or was he talking that way deliberately? Trying to hurt her? She remembered the darkness she had seen in his eyes in the garden, the ice edging his voice, and shivered.

What did she know about him now, anyway? Three years was a long time. Ritchie had visibly changed—what invisible changes had there been? What went on inside his head?

She watched him walking across her bedroom totally naked: she couldn't take her eyes off the broad shoulders, long, smooth back, the muscled legs with their rough, dark hair along the calves. He moved with such an impatient, unselfconscious, masculine grace, and Linzi felt very weird, having him there, in her bedroom. He acted as if he belonged there, as if he was absolutely at home, but Linzi couldn't adjust to the intimacy of the situation.

Without a backward glance he walked into the bathroom, closed the door. A second later she heard the shower start.

She scrambled off the bed and pulled a cotton dressing-gown out of her wardrobe, put it on with shaky hands, tied the frilled belt with a large bow just as Ritchie came back into the bedroom with a bath-towel tied around his waist, his bare, damp shoulders gleaming in the late afternoon sunlight.

Her throat closed up. No man should be that sexy, it wasn't fair. She had to look away, swallowing. If only she knew why he was acting this way. What had their lovemaking really meant to him? He had talked about needing her, wanting her . . . she tried to remember him using the word love, and couldn't. Why had he been so determined to find her? To make her admit she was in love with him? To get her into bed?

Megan had warned her that Ritchie was bitter, might come looking for her to get some sort of angry revenge. Was that it?

Linzi's stomach clenched in sick shame. Had he set out to seduce her just to get revenge?

He was carrying his clothes; she watched him drop them on the end of the bed while he put on his wrist-watch and turned to her dressing-table to run a comb through his wet hair.

In the mirror his reflected eyes skated to Linzi, absorbed the fact that she was now wearing a full-length, long-sleeved dressing-gown with a high ruff neck, a sash belt tied tightly around her waist.

His brows arched in mockery. 'Very Victorian. I preferred you the way you were.'

Pink flowered in her face; she looked away, her hands clenched at her sides, wanting to hit him.

Ritchie laughed, then began to dress with quick, economical movements.

Linzi summoned up her last remnant of pride and walked out of the room without a word. He was making it insultingly clear that the way they'd made love had meant nothing to him, it had all been a game to him. OK, two could play at that game. She wasn't bursting into tears, pleading with him, allowing him the satisfaction of seeing her on her knees.

She went downstairs, into the kitchen, and filled the kettle, put it on the hob. As she got a cup and saucer down she heard the whir of the helicopter and looked out of the window in time to see it descending into the field just in front of the cottage, whipping the tall grass into a whirlpool of green ears and bending stems. Ted could put down on a sixpence, he often said, but she was always impressed by his skill.

Thinking of Ted made her blush suddenly. He wouldn't come to the cottage, would he? If he saw her in her dressing-gown, guessed she had been to bed with Ritchie, she would want to die of embarrassment. He would go back and tell Megan. Linzi put her hands against her hot face, stifling a groan.

Behind her she heard a firm step and tensed, not daring to turn round or face him.

'I'll walk over and meet Ted,' Ritchie said brusquely. 'I won't bring him back here. We'll take off right away.'

She nodded, not risking her voice in case she broke into tears. Was he really leaving like this? He must hate her to want to hurt her this much.

She heard him stride out of the room, through the hall, slamming the front door behind him a moment later. From the window she watched as he ran across the lane into the field. A few moments later the helicopter took off again, the blades rotating, the grass bending and blowing in that circular motion. Linzi watched them fly into the blue haze of the late spring day, their black shadow following them across the fields below.

The kettle boiled. The kitchen filled with steam and the sound of whistling. Linzi was crying so much that she couldn't move for a minute, then she made herself go over to switch off the heat under the kettle. Like an automaton she made herself instant black coffee and sat down with the mug in her shaking hands.

How could she have let this happen to her? If Ritchie had come here for revenge he had certainly got it. Humiliation welled up inside her; she bit her lip until she tasted blood.

Would he be back? He hadn't said and she had refused to humiliate herself by asking. But one thing was certain—she wasn't staying here, waiting for Ritchie. As soon as she could pull herself together she was leaving, packing everything back into her car and clearing out. But where should she go? That was the question.

If she went back to Aunt Ella and the antiques shop Ritchie would know where to find her any time he chose. She had money saved, she could find a new home, a new job, and start again, somewhere else.

Yet why should she? Why should she let Ritchie drive her away from a place she liked, a job she had learnt to love? From the only family she had left in the world? She had grown very fond of Aunt Ella and Gareth and little Paul, she didn't want to lose touch with them again, and she knew they would be just as sad at such a prospect.

Maybe she should talk it over with them? If Ritchie was going to London to dinner he wouldn't be back tonight, if he ever did come back! She had time to discuss her future with Aunt Ella and Gareth, take their advice as to what she should do next.

She finished her coffee and went upstairs to start packing. It didn't take long, as she had very little with her and she could get it all into a couple of cases and a few cardboard boxes.

She carried the cases out to the little garage and packed them into her car, then went back for the cardboard boxes. She must leave the cottage in perfect condition for the real owner, so she spent an hour tidying and cleaning, and felt quite weary by the time she finally locked up the house.

By then darkness had fallen, and out here in the countryside the darkness was blacker than it was in towns and cities, where the streets sent up a glow of sulphurous yellow into the night sky. Once Linzi had switched off the lights in the cottage the garden became dangerous territory, a black jungle full of whispering grasses and creeping sounds.

She had to feel her way back to the garage. With a sigh of relief she switched on the lights inside the garage, opened her car door and got behind the wheel. She switched on the ignition.

Nothing happened.

She looked blankly at the dashboard panel, then turned her key again. Nothing. Not a sign of life.

She looked at the petrol gauge. Nearly full of petrol. She went through the various easy checks she had learnt to make. She was no mechanic, but sometimes it could be something simple that was easy to detect. In this case it was obviously something serious because there was not a flicker of life from the engine.

The battery must be dead, she decided, and got the bonnet open to look underneath it rather hopelessly. She didn't have a spare battery and no set of jump leads to start the battery off again, and she couldn't even ring up a garage to come and start the car for her.

But she looked into the engine anyway, in the hope of inspiration. That was when she discovered that the plugs were missing. She stared at the trailing leads, her mouth open in a gasp of rage.

She knew at once, of course, what had happened. Ritchie had removed them. It was a fiendishly clever but simple way of immobilising the car because she didn't have a spare set of plugs, either, but it would only have taken Ritchie a minute to take the four plugs out. No doubt they were in his jeans pocket right now as he flew off to London.

He might have thrown them away, into the garden— but in this darkness she hadn't a hope in hell of finding them.

She was stuck here. She slammed the bonnet down and unloaded her cases, grimly took everything back into the cottage and locked doors, bolted windows, making sure there was no possible way Ritchie could get back into the house before morning.

At first light she would be up and she would start walking to the nearest village. She would go tonight, if she wasn't afraid of walking there in the dark, along lonely country roads. Her nerves were already shot to pieces. This had been a very difficult day and it wasn't over yet. Linzi didn't feel she could face any more trauma. So she made herself a little scrambled egg, had some fruit and a glass of milk and went to bed, but first she locked her bedroom door.

Ritchie wasn't getting anywhere near her again.

CHAPTER NINE

AMAZINGLY, Linzi did get to sleep, although she had been afraid she wouldn't. Exhaustion caught up with her within minutes of getting into bed; when her alarm went at five o'clock she practically hit the roof in shock and stumbled out of bed still only half conscious, yawning, flushed, drowsy-eyed.

For a second she was totally disoriented. She stood beside her bed blinking at the clock.

Five o'clock. What on earth ...?

Then she remembered. She had set it for five so that she would be up at dawn to walk to the next village and ring for a taxi. She intended to go to the nearest garage, buy some spark plugs and come back here for her car before Ritchie got here.

If he was coming! He might have no such intention—but if not, why had he immobilised her car, stranding her here?

She hurried into the bathroom to shower in lukewarm water. It would wake her up fully. At the moment she felt as if she was sleepwalking. She would skip breakfast, just have coffee, she decided, as she dressed five minutes later, in thin white cotton jeans and a deep blue cotton sweater. She slid her feet into white trainers and brushed her silky, damp hair, then went downstairs.

She made instant coffee and drank it standing in the kitchen, staring out into the garden, her face sombre, blue eyes set and haunted. She wouldn't let herself remember what had happened yesterday between her and Ritchie, yet the memories were there all the time behind a dam, the weight of them threatening to overwhelm her if once they broke free.

Shivering, she finished her coffee and washed up the cup, dried it, put it away, moving like a robot around the kitchen. Pain had become a dull, permanent ache behind her eyes; if she kept busy she could ignore it.

The light was flooding into the sky by the time she set out. There was a stillness in the air, a waiting for the day to begin, the first few sleepy calls of birds, a whisper of bending grass and moving branches in the wood.

Linzi didn't share the pleasurable anticipation of the natural world at the opening of another day. She looked bleakly up at the glimmering sky as she locked the front door of the cottage behind her, wishing she didn't feel so grey and weary. She was certainly in no mood to enjoy a long, invigorating walk! What she really felt like doing was going back to bed for another six hours.

She set off along the rough unmade track between fields which led eventually to the main road to Warwick. There were deep ruts in the surface here and there. She kept missing her step, stumbling. She had to look down, watch where she put her feet.

She had gone a few hundred yards when a horse rode out of the woodland on the right. Linzi might have spotted it sooner if she hadn't had her gaze fixed on the path. As it was the first she knew of it was the creak of saddle leather, the rustle of grasses as the animal headed towards her.

Startled, she looked round, saw the big black horse, looked up at the rider and drew a shaky breath.

Ritchie!

Linzi's heart began to thud into her ribs. For a moment she was too taken aback at seeing him to do more than stare, frozen in her tracks.

It had only taken one glance to recognise his hard face in the shadow of a black velvet riding hat. She had no idea he ever rode, but he clearly knew what he was doing; he rode with effortless, casual grace, his long back straight, his body moving as if he were one with the horse. He wasn't dressed specifically for horse riding; he was just wearing a yellow polo-neck sweater, jeans and brown boots, but they were perfectly suitable.

She took all that in with searing intensity, at the same time managing to see the glitter of Ritchie's grey eyes, the angry set of jaw and mouth, as he galloped towards her.

In a panic she began to run along the track, although how she hoped to get away from him she couldn't really have said. Instinct simply made her bolt for it, and when she heard Ritchie's horse behind her, hoofs beating in the dusty road, so that she felt the vibrations in her own body, she swerved out of his way up the bank topped by a hedge, into the field beyond.

Her heart was beating up in her throat by then, her lungs laboured, dragging in air roughly, and adrenalin made her run faster than she would ever have thought she could.

She felt like a fox being hunted, except that there was no pack of hounds baying behind her, only a man on a tall horse, a man with a dark, formidable face, who came on relentlessly, closer and closer, until he rode level with her, his mount barely inches away from her shoulder.

Ritchie leaned down. She gave him a terrified glance, her blue eyes dilated, her skin overheated with the effort of her flight. His hand shot out, curling round her waist before she could get away. She felt his arm tightening on her body, then she was being lifted up off the ground, feet kicking.

As soon as she realised what he meant to do she began to struggle, attempting to break out of the hold he had on her.

Ritchie exerted pressure, trying to drag her on to his horse, which, alarmed, plunged sideways, snorting. Linzi was swinging in mid-air, breathlessly wriggling to make Ritchie let go of her. He tried to calm his mount, his knees gripping the animal's sides, one hand holding the reins while the other still held Linzi, but the horse was in a state of sudden panic. It bucked, hind legs kicking out, and Ritchie was thrown forward.

Surprise made him loosen his grip on Linzi. She gave a high-pitched cry of alarm as she felt herself start to fall. The ground seemed a long way away.

Ritchie grabbed at her instinctively and caught her by the shoulders, then the law of gravity came into operation and the weight of her body made her slip out of his grasp, his hand sliding through her silky hair, gripping her nape.

At the same instant the horse bolted.

Ritchie was thrown, heavily. He took Linzi with him; landed on top of her, still grasping her by the throat.

The back of Linzi's head hit the ground hard; she half lost consciousness, her body limp underneath Ritchie.

Coming back to awareness, she opened dazed eyes and began to scream.

Ritchie sat up, looking down at her with anxiety in his hard grey eyes.

'Linzi, what is it? Are you badly hurt?'

She was white as a ghost, her blue eyes like deep, dark wells as she stared upwards, and Ritchie was shaken by that look in her face, by the wildness of her screaming. 'What on earth is it, Linzi? Where does it hurt? Stop screaming, darling, tell me what's wrong.'

He shook her gently, but she went on making that terrible noise, as if she couldn't stop. Ritchie began feeling her arms and legs, testing for injuries. He couldn't find anything obvious: no broken bones at all, a couple of dark red bruises on one arm where she had fallen on it, a few light scratches. Nothing that could explain the way she was screaming.

'For God's sake, Linzi!' Ritchie was pale too, his face disturbed. 'Does your head hurt? Stop screaming and listen. How can I help you if you won't tell me what's wrong?' He looked at her set, rigid white face. 'Linzi, you're hysterical! I'm sorry about this, but if you won't stop I shall have to make you!'

He slapped her around the face.

Linzi stopped on a breath, and then began to cry, tears streaming down her face.

'Well, tears are better than that terrifying noise!' he said drily, and took her in his arms as if she were a child, began to rock her against him, holding her very close, his chin on her hair. 'Sssh...sssh...calm down, darling, and tell me where it hurts. I'll get you to a doctor right away. My car is parked behind some trees two minutes from here.'

'I...' she chokily sobbed. 'I...'

'Yes, darling, go on,' he urged, stroking her hair with one hand, still rocking her rhythmically, her body lying in his lap, across his legs. 'What hurts?'

'I did it,' she sobbed. 'Didn't I? It was me...not you...'

Ritchie stiffened, his hand stilling as it smoothed down her hair, his face white, tense, shadowed. 'What? What are you talking about?'

'I killed Barty!' she whispered, the tears still running down her cheeks.

Ritchie sat up straighter, tilted her head back over his arm, her long pale hair falling in a curtain of shimmering silk. He looked down carefully into her tear-stained face. 'What do you mean, Linzi?'

Wildly she cried, 'I killed him, it wasn't you at all. I hit him with that candlestick...'

Ritchie gave a long, hard sigh. 'You've remembered.'

Her darkened eyes stared at him sightlessly, her face drawn with shock. Her teeth had begun to chatter and she was shivering violently, her body very cold.

'It's true, isn't it? I did it. I don't understand... I can't understand how I forgot!' She looked at him, agitated, distressed. 'I didn't know, Ritchie, I wasn't lying,

I simply didn't remember doing it, until just now, when it hit me suddenly, out of the blue...'

He stroked back the tangled silvery hair from her face, his eyes soothing, tender. 'Calm down, Linzi, nobody's accusing you.'

She stared at him incredulously, her eyes searching his face. 'But why didn't you say anything?' she whispered. 'You went through that whole trial and you never said a word, not even to me! But you knew it was me who'd done it, you knew you hadn't! Why on earth didn't you tell the police it was me?'

He didn't answer that. 'When did you remember?' he asked. 'Just now when you fell? Maybe you hit your head and——'

She shook her head, still shivering. 'No. I remembered before I actually hit the ground. I suddenly remembered when you caught me just now, when I felt your hand round my throat...it was *déjà vu*...I remembered that night then...' She gave a violent shudder. 'It was so vivid...as if it was happening again. For a second I got you both confused, you and Barty...he was holding me by the throat that night, he pulled me up off the floor by my throat, that was when I knew he was going to kill me, I was choking, everything was going black...and...and...'

Her voice was quivering, very high, the words coming out jerkily, and Ritchie watched her with frowning anxiety.

'Linzi, slow down, stop talking for a minute and breathe slowly...you must calm down; don't get hysterical again.'

She took a long, painful breath, trembling, then whispered, 'I didn't know what to do, you see, couldn't think...except to keep saying to myself, He's going to kill me, Barty's going to kill me, I'm going to die, this is what dying feels like! And suddenly I didn't want to die. I wanted to live. I think I went a little crazy myself, I clawed at him like an animal, trying to make him let go, and he knocked my hand away. As it fell down it brushed against the candlestick and I grabbed it instinctively and...and hit him...'

Her voice trailed away and she groaned, closing her eyes.

Ritchie groaned, too, kissed her lids, her wet cheeks, her hair. 'Darling, don't think about it any more, you worry me when you look like that...'

She didn't seem to hear him. The hoarse jerky voice went on, 'I hit him as hard as I could and I heard him give this funny deep moan, and he let go of me, he fell down, and I must have fainted, because I don't remember anything after that, until I came to and you were there, and Barty was...' She stopped, her hand to her trembling lips, choking back sobs, then turned her face into his chest and wept into his shirt.

Ritchie silently comforted her, his face against her hair, until the sound of weeping slowed and stopped. With a long, wrenched sigh, she lifted her head and looked up at him, her wild blue eyes bewildered, dazed. 'Ritchie, you knew...you knew you hadn't done it, for God's sake, why didn't you tell the police the truth? Why did you let them charge you?'

He shrugged, his face rueful. 'At first I was too stunned to think, I was in shock, too, having walked in to find your husband dead on the floor and you half dead too. Then you started yelling that I'd killed him, and you looked at me as if you hated me, and said it was all my fault, he wouldn't have been dead if it hadn't been for me, and somehow I didn't care what happened to me for a while.'

She closed her eyes, groaning. 'Oh, Ritchie...oh, I'm so sorry...what can I say to you? I was so unhappy and confused, I was feeling so guilty myself and I really did think you had done it, God knows why...I suppose I was subconsciously just looking for someone else to blame, I couldn't bear to face the fact that I had killed him.'

'I worked that out,' he said drily. 'I didn't realise then that you had genuinely forgotten, I thought it was just the first effects of shock and trauma, and that in a few hours, a day or so, you would tell the police the truth and then I meant to get you the best lawyers money could buy. I was sure no court would convict you. It was a clear case of self-defence. He was trying to kill you, he'd been beating you up for a long time, and I agree with you, that last time he would probably have killed you. It was self-defence, you had no choice. Survival is a very strong human instinct.'

She covered her face with her shaking hands. 'But I never meant to, it was...just a sort of reflex action...I had to stop him and I couldn't because he was much stronger than me, and I was so scared of him when he was in one of his drunken rages! I just wanted to stop him, you see, I didn't want to hurt him, let alone kill him!'

'Nobody would blame you, Linzi. Nobody!' Ritchie said, his voice gentle, taking her hands away and kissing the palms lightly. 'I certainly didn't.'

She sobbed. 'Don't! Oh, I feel so awful! I let you take the blame! Why did you let me do that? You should have told the police!'

He gave her a crooked little smile. 'Much as I would like to play the noble martyr, it wasn't quite like that. I never meant to be noble, I just kept my mouth shut and waited, expecting you to admit what had happened, and then I began to realise you weren't going to!'

She bit her lip in anguish. 'Oh... when I think... how on earth must you have felt? What a terrible position to be in! I still don't understand why you didn't tell the police the truth!'

He looked into her eyes and softly said, 'Well, you see, I was in love with you...'

A little colour crept back into her face, her face quivered with sudden feeling. 'Oh, Ritchie...'

He smiled. 'It didn't take long for me to guess you must have some sort of amnesia.'

'I might have been lying, though, trying to put all the blame on you!'

He shook his head, smiling properly. 'I knew you too well to think that. No, I worked out that killing Barty had been so traumatic for you that your conscious mind couldn't face the fact that you'd done it. Your unconscious was protecting your sanity by wiping out the memory of what really happened.'

She was frowning uncertainly. 'Ritchie...at the trial...they said your fingerprints were on the candlestick, on top of a set of mine...you must have touched it after I did...after...'

'I took it out of your hand,' he said, his eyes sombre.

She winced, groaned. 'I was still holding it?'

He nodded.

Whiter than ever, she whispered, 'You should have told the police, Ritchie! You shouldn't have taken the blame.'

He shrugged. 'If you had had to face the truth, so soon afterwards, you might have gone out of your mind. Your unconscious had protected you from the memory by blanking it out altogether. Once I'd faced up to that, I knew I couldn't force you to remember. It might have been disastrous for your mental state. I wasn't going to see you taken off to a mental hospital, or prison, when you were in such a frail condition.'

'Oh, Ritchie,' she whispered, utterly shaken. 'You went to prison for me, and I told you I never wanted to see you again, I said I hated you!' She remembered the way she had talked to him, looked at him, and was appalled.

His mouth twisted ironically. 'That wasn't easy to take, no! I had stopped expecting you to confess by then, but I had thought you would stand by me while I was going through the trial, maybe even doing a prison sentence. You might believe I'd killed your husband, but as far as you knew I'd done it for you, after all! I thought you would visit me in prison, that we'd stay in touch, and when I came out you would be waiting for me.'

She bit her lip. 'No wonder you were so angry with me! You must have hated me!'

His black lashes cloaked his eyes and he smiled slowly. 'I had some very violent feelings towards you, it's true, but I didn't hate you, Linzi. You can't really have thought I ever did.'

Their eyes met and she blushed, remembering yesterday, the wild, burning passion of those moments in her bed. She looked down, her lashes fluttering, her breathing very fast. 'You should have hated me! I couldn't blame you if you had.'

Ritchie caught her face between his hands, tilted her head to make her look up at him, stared deep into her startled blue eyes. 'I love you, Linzi,' he muttered passionately.

'Ritchie...' she breathed, her lips apart, quivering, and his stare dropped to them, fixed on them intensely. Slowly he bent to kiss them, his eyes closing, heat growing between the two of them.

'Linzi...oh, God, Linzi, I love you more than my life,' he muttered, and her arm curled round his neck, caressed his nape, her fingers twisting into his short, dark hair.

He lifted his mouth, breathing thickly. 'Unless you want to make love here, in this field, I think we'd better start walking.'

Hot colour blazed into her face.

'We'll go to my car, use the car phone to make an emergency appointment for you to see a doctor—I want you thoroughly checked over, in case you have an injury of some kind after that fall.'

'I'm fine,' she protested. 'It was shock, not an injury, that made me remember.'

'Well, anyway, I want to make sure you're OK,' Ritchie insisted, getting to his feet and pulling her up with him. 'And I must ring the stables and tell them what has happened. That stupid horse has probably gone straight back there, and they might send out a search party for me, in case I was thrown and injured. They're going to laugh like hyenas. I told them I was a highly experienced rider! And then to get thrown, like a novice! I shall never be able to show my face there again.'

She gave a faint smile. 'That will teach you to hunt women down and try to drag them on to your horse!'

He laughed, unrepentant. 'So it will!' She was a little unsteady on her feet; his face changed, and he looked at her anxiously. 'Maybe you should sit down and I'll get my car and come and pick you up.'

'I'm fine,' she insisted.

He put an arm around her waist and she leaned on him a little as they began to walk along the lane.

His car was hidden, as he had said, behind a little plantation of young trees on the edge of the wood. Ritchie unhooked his car phone and made a brief call, laughing at whatever the person at the other end said to him.

'Well, I'm glad he got back safely,' he murmured. 'I'll let you know in advance next time I want a ride. See you.'

He rang off, looked at her with one eyebrow raised. 'Now, what's your doctor's number around here?'

'I've no idea, and I don't want to see a doctor, Ritchie!'

He looked at her uncertainly. 'I think you should. Why don't we go up to London and make an appointment for you to see a good Harley Street man?'

'Maybe tomorrow,' she compromised, and with that he had to be satisfied.

He slid her into the front passenger seat, got behind the wheel and drove back to the cottage.

'That reminds me, Ritchie,' she said, suddenly remembering, 'where are my sparking plugs? I want them back! I ought to have called the police and reported you for such a lowdown, sneaking trick!'

'Except that you had no phone!' he told her, grinning. 'Were you furious when you realised what I'd done?'

'Furious!' she said, but laughed.

'It was all I could think of, to keep you there. I was afraid you'd run away again if I left you alone, that I'd get back to find the cottage empty and you gone. I didn't want to start hunting for you all over again. So I tried to make it difficult for you to leave, although I couldn't make it impossible. I hoped that by the time you discovered the car wouldn't start it would be too late for you to start walking to the nearest phone.'

She looked at him through her lashes, her face altering, a questioning look in her blue eyes. 'But why did you leave at all, after...?' She broke off, blushing, and he laughed softly.

'After the way we made love?' He pulled up outside her cottage and turned to look at her, passion in his eyes.

She found it hard to hold his gaze, her face full of scalding colour. 'You were so offhand afterwards, so curt and distant!' she reproached him. 'Why did you change like that, then leave so abruptly? I thought you had seduced me just to get some sort of revenge on me. After you'd gone I felt so miserable!'

'Linzi, you can't have thought that!' He sounded shocked, shaken. 'After the way we'd made love? My God, don't you know how I felt after that? I could barely walk, let alone speak. Just breathing was an effort. What I'd wanted to do was fall asleep in your arms, but I had to get up and dress and fly back to London with Ted, but believe me it was one of the hardest things I've ever done in my life.'

Her heart beat fiercely behind her ribs. Breathlessly she asked him, 'But why couldn't you tell me that? Why did you go without really even looking at me?'

'If I had looked at you I'd have got straight back into bed and made love to you again,' he said hoarsely, sending waves of heat through her.

'Oh...' she said.

He laughed. 'Yes. Oh. Linzi, I had to leave you last night. It meant the difference between losing my company and keeping it.'

She gave a start of shock. 'What do you mean? You aren't serious?'

'Deadly,' he clipped out, his mouth hard.

'But... I don't understand—how could that happen? Nobody could take your company away from you. You're the biggest shareholder, aren't you?'

His face held irony, cynicism. 'Yes, but, although it is a private company, the other shareholders could have got together to vote me off the board; there was a very strong possibility that that might happen.'

'But why?'

He shrugged. 'While I was in prison the new chairman was Roger Jeffrey; he has got used to being in the seat of power and doesn't want to give it up. He was engineering a *coup d'état*.'

'Oh, no!' Linzi was shocked. So someone else had betrayed him? And this time for such greedy reasons. 'After all you'd been through! How could he? I thought he was your friend.'

'I thought so too. But ambitious men forget friendship overnight. Luckily, I got wind of it through Ted, who keeps his ear close to the ground. He flies the executives all the time; he overheard something, and tipped me off. I've always been able to trust Ted to the hilt. I knew I had to act myself, before they made their move. There was only one way I could do it—make a pact with the other major shareholder. You remember old Mrs Evans, who lives in Portugal most of the year?'

She gave him a startled look. 'She came into the office one day, didn't she? A very old woman with white hair and masses of rings on her hands.'

Ritchie gave a bark of laughter. 'Women notice the oddest things! But yes, that's Amy. She's a very rich woman, too. Her husband left her a big block of my shares when he died. She almost never comes back to England, but her husband was one of my father's closest colleagues for years. I've known her most of my life, and I knew if I talked to her face to face I could persuade her to back me up. That was what I was doing last night over dinner. She had been so shocked when I went to prison for manslaughter that Jeffrey and his conspirators had been able to talk her into voting with them against me, but once I was able to talk to her face to face I managed to swing her back to my side. She's over seventy, and doesn't understand business—she offered to sell me her shares, though, and I've jumped at the chance.'

Linzi had met Roger Jeffrey. The man was short, balding, with acquisitive eyes and a secret smile; she had not liked him.

In bleak tones she said, 'It never seems to stop, does it? After everything you've gone through for my sake to have lost your company too would have been the last straw, wouldn't it?'

'No,' he said huskily. 'The last straw would be to lose you, Linzi.'

Her eyes were wide and brilliant with feeling. 'Ritchie!'

His answering gaze was intense, a dark, passionate brooding. 'If I had to choose between you and the company I wouldn't even hesitate. I can always start up in business again, if I have to—but I could never find another woman like you.'

Tears welled up in her eyes again, she gave a choked little sob. 'Oh, Ritchie...you make me feel so...I don't deserve to be loved like that.'

'You're the loveliest thing I've ever seen,' he said huskily. 'I could no more stop loving you than I could stop breathing. You were all I thought about while I was in prison. I was desperate to get out of there simply so that I could find you. I was very worried about you: I thought you might be living on the edge of a volcano, that at any minute the amnesia block might break and you would be forced to realise the truth, and I was afraid of what that might do to you. I wanted to be there, when it happened, to make sure the realisation didn't destroy you.'

She closed her eyes, a sigh torn from her. 'It is terrible, isn't it? Even though I never meant to kill him I still did. No wonder I've been living with this heavy sense of guilt. I thought I was guilty over how I felt about you, but it wasn't just that, was it? I might have blocked the truth out, but somewhere in my mind I think I knew what really happened.'

'The unconscious plays some very odd tricks,' Ritchie agreed. 'It might be a good idea for you to see an analyst—a course of therapy might help you come to terms with all this. Walking around carrying a massive load of guilt could make havoc for the rest of your life if you don't deal with it soon.'

She nodded. 'I'll make sure I deal with it. And I must tell the police too.'

'No!' Ritchie firmly said. 'There's no need to tell them anything.'

'But it's important to tell the truth, set the record straight...'

'The debt has been paid,' Ritchie said. 'I paid it for you, and I don't want you to pay again.'

'But——' she prompted and he put a finger on her lips, the coolness of his flesh against hers sending a shudder of sensitive awareness through her whole body.

'No buts. I'm deadly serious. You are not to tell the police—nor anyone else!'

She looked uncertainly at him, frowning. 'I think I should...'

'No. If you told them, the police might feel forced to charge you; after all, they would have to admit they'd made a mistake, sent the wrong person to prison, so they would have to take steps to put matters right, wouldn't they? There was only one crime—why should two people pay the price for it? I've paid the debt to society and I don't want you paying too. So promise me, Linzi, promise me you won't tell anyone else what really happened.'

'But I owe it to you above all!' she said unhappily.

Ritchie shook his head, his face hard and insistent.

'Linzi, do as I ask, please. Promise me you won't breathe a word about any of this, except to the analyst we get you!'

She gave a husky sigh. 'I owe Barty the truth, too, Ritchie!'

'You don't owe him anything.' He stroked her hair back from her distressed, uncertain face. 'And I'm certain that if he was here now he'd say the same to you. You made him a good wife, you went on loving him long after many women would have given up on him, you tried to stay faithful and loyal when he had stepped beyond the bounds of the tolerable, and you put up with some stuff from him that you shouldn't have had to bear.

But Barty died three years ago, darling. It's time to bury him, forget the bad times and remember the good times, show him a little loving tenderness and say goodbye without any more bitterness or guilt. Let him rest in peace. Now that you know the truth I think you'll find it easier to do that.'

She slowly nodded, her lip tremulous. 'My guilt held me back from saying goodbye to him all this time.'

'Yes,' he said simply.

She gave another long sigh. 'Oh, Ritchie, I wonder you can bear to talk to me, after all the pain I caused you!'

'I love you,' he said quietly, then he opened the car door and came round to help her out, bent his dark head to kiss her mouth briefly, possessively. 'Come inside now and let me show you just how much I love you,' he whispered against her mouth.

She felt her heart turn over. The passion in his voice was spellbinding. Her mouth aching and burning from his kiss, she let him walk her towards the house, his arm around her waist, his step urgent, hurrying. The same fierce urgency possessed her. She couldn't wait to make love to him, she felt the hot need aching inside her body and her breathing was difficult. This time would be different; this time there would be no barriers of guilt and shame between her and Ritchie.

She lifted her glowing eyes to the blue sky. The sun was fully up now. Birds were singing in the Warwickshire wood; bluebells spread their blue mist under the oak and ash and beech trees. The bright day had begun; the world seemed newly minted. Linzi felt so light that she could almost have floated away into the cloudless sky...finally free of the dark shadows of the past which had held her captive for so long.

HARLEQUIN®

PRESENTS *plus*

When Prince Uzziah invited Beth back to his sumptuous palace, she thought he was about to sell her the Arab stallion of her dreams. But Uzziah had another deal on his mind—a race...where the winner took all....

Kelda had always clashed with her stepbrother, Angelo, but now he was interfering in her life. He claimed it was for family reasons, and he demanded Kelda enter into a new relationship with him—as his mistress!

What would you do if *you* were Beth or Kelda? Share their pleasure and their passion—watch for:

Beth and the Barbarian by Miranda Lee
Harlequin Presents Plus #1711

and

Angel of Darkness by Lynne Graham
Harlequin Presents Plus #1712

Harlequin Presents Plus
The best has just gotten better!

Available in January wherever Harlequin books are sold.

MILLION DOLLAR SWEEPSTAKES (III)

No purchase necessary. To enter, follow the directions published. Method of entry may vary. For eligibility, entries must be received no later than March 31, 1996. No liability is assumed for printing errors, lost, late or misdirected entries. Odds of winning are determined by the number of eligible entries distributed and received. Prizewinners will be determined no later than June 30, 1996.

Sweepstakes open to residents of the U.S. (except Puerto Rico), Canada, Europe and Taiwan who are 18 years of age or older. All applicable laws and regulations apply. Sweepstakes offer void wherever prohibited by law. Values of all prizes are in U.S. currency. This sweepstakes is presented by Torstar Corp., its subsidiaries and affiliates, in conjunction with book, merchandise and/or product offerings. For a copy of the Official Rules send a self-addressed, stamped envelope (WA residents need not affix return postage) to: MILLION DOLLAR SWEEPSTAKES (III) Rules, P.O. Box 4573, Blair, NE 68009, USA.

EXTRA BONUS PRIZE DRAWING

No purchase necessary. The Extra Bonus Prize will be awarded in a random drawing to be conducted no later than 5/30/96 from among all entries received. To qualify, entries must be received by 3/31/96 and comply with published directions. Drawing open to residents of the U.S. (except Puerto Rico), Canada, Europe and Taiwan who are 18 years of age or older. All applicable laws and regulations apply; offer void wherever prohibited by law. Odds of winning are dependent upon number of eligibile entries received. Prize is valued in U.S. currency. The offer is presented by Torstar Corp., its subsidiaries and affiliates in conjunction with book, merchandise and/or product offering. For a copy of the Official Rules governing this sweepstakes, send a self-addressed, stamped envelope (WA residents need not affix return postage) to: Extra Bonus Prize Drawing Rules, P.O. Box 4590, Blair, NE 68009, USA.

SWP-H1294

If you are looking for more titles by

CHARLOTTE LAMB

Don't miss these fabulous stories by one of
Harlequin's great authors:

Harlequin Presents®

#11370	DARK PURSUIT	$2.75	☐
#11467	HEART ON FIRE	$2.89	☐
#11480	SHOTGUN WEDDING	$2.89	☐
#11560	SLEEPING PARTNERS	$2.99	☐
#11584	FORBIDDEN FRUIT	$2.99	☐
#11618	DREAMING	$2.99	☐

(The following titles are part of the Barbary Wharf series)

#11498	BESIEGED	$2.89	☐
#11509	BATTLE FOR POSSESSION	$2.89	☐
#11530	A SWEET ADDICTION	$2.89	☐
#11540	SURRENDER	$2.89	☐

(limited quantities available on certain titles)

TOTAL AMOUNT	$
POSTAGE & HANDLING	$
($1.00 for one book, 50¢ for each additional)	
APPLICABLE TAXES*	$_____
TOTAL PAYABLE	$_____

(check or money order—please do not send cash)

To order, complete this form and send it, along with a check or money order
for the total above, payable to Harlequin Books, to: **In the U.S.:** 3010 Walden
Avenue, P.O. Box 9047, Buffalo, NY 14269-9047; **In Canada:** P.O. Box 613,
Fort Erie, Ontario, L2A 5X3.

Name:_____

Address:_____ City:_____

State/Prov.:_____ Zip/Postal Code:_____

*New York residents remit applicable sales taxes.
 Canadian residents remit applicable GST and provincial taxes.   HCLBACK2

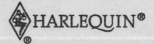
HARLEQUIN®